LIFEMAKER

BOOKS BY DEAN F. WILSON

THE CHILDREN OF TELM

Book One: The Call of Agon
Book Two: The Road to Rebirth
Book Three: The Chains of War

THE GREAT IRON WAR

Hopebreaker
Lifemaker
Skyshaker

THE GREAT IRON WAR - BOOK TWO

LIFEMAKER

DEAN F. WILSON

Cover illustration by Duy Phan

First Edition 2015

ISBN 978-1-909356-10-8

DIOSCURI PRESS

Published by Dioscuri Press
Dublin, Ireland

www.dioscuripress.com
enquiries@dioscuripress.com

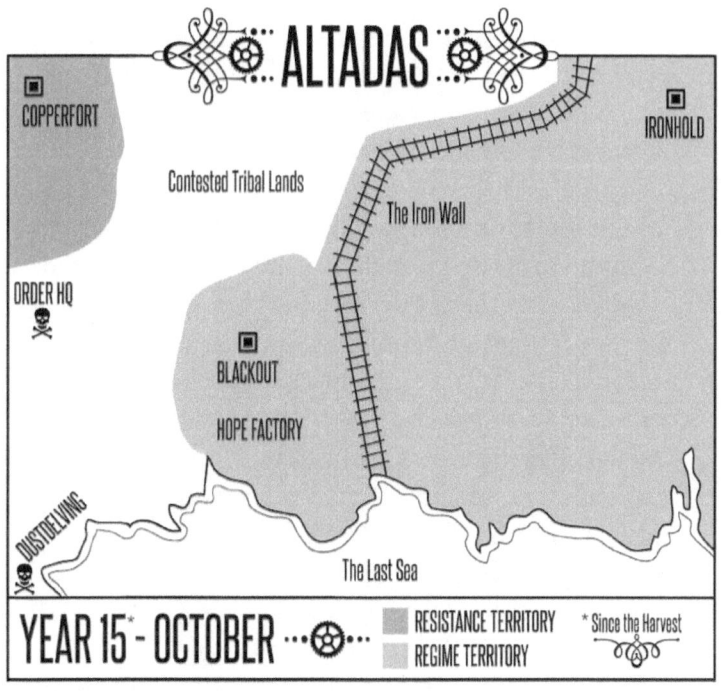

THE GREAT IRON WAR

In the world of Altadas, in the year 1888 of the Second Era, women everywhere dreamed of a coming desert. Those who were already pregnant miscarried, and those who became pregnant did not give birth to human children. An invasion had begun.

The newborns had no horns or marks, and so they were loved and reared like all the others. It would take time before anyone realised what they really were, before anyone would call them demons.

These events were marked by the arrival of strangers claiming to be from a distant land. The people of Altadas called them Pilgrims, but they did not know just how far they had come, nor by what strange doors they had entered, nor exactly what they had come for.

The first Pilgrims were scouts, but subsequent waves were soldiers, sent by a man who would later call himself the Iron Emperor. He promised his people iron. He gave them war instead.

They called that year the Harvest, and it became the first year of a new, darker calendar. Sand swept through the great chasms in the sky from where the demons came, the dust of a world that they had dried up. Ahead of the landships went great sandstorms, until the green grasses became an endless red desert.

In Altadas, steam powers industry, but iron powers

war. The abundant metal, idolised by the invaders, and depleted in their home world, became a beacon to the demons, and was the foundation upon which they would build their new civilisation. They called themselves the Iron Empire. Their enemies simply called them the Regime.

As war began in the east, few among the Resistance knew that their own children were not really theirs. The invaders had mastered a magical technique to control the birth channels of a people they desired to conquer. Thus with one hand they would wield might, and with the other they would use guile, infiltrating and eradicating their enemies, anyone who would dare defy the Iron Emperor, who had brought his people to this promised land.

Yet iron is more to the demons than just a metal. When broken down into its basic elements, it provides the key ingredient of the necessary sustenance of the invaders. To some it is a drug. To them, symbolising everything they were promised, and everything they were leaving behind, it is Hope.

As one civilisation crumbled, and a new empire was founded on its remains, there were some who refused to live out their last days under the iron grip of their new ruler. They made a promise of their own: to fight, with everything they had, for the fate of humanity.

Thus began the Great Iron War.

CONTENTS

Chapter

Chapter One

DESCENT

The submarine's dive alarm rang out its ear-piercing siren within seconds of the final hatch being shut and sealed. Its repetitive drone made Jacob feel like bailing out, but maybe it had more to do with the fact that it was also the final warning before the ocean became his prison.

"Clear the bridge," Rommond ordered. Jacob had already been ushered outside, and he thought it was a personal slight until he found everyone else, the general included, coming out to join him.

"Nice of you to keep me company," Jacob said, but Rommond was too preoccupied to take notice.

A flood of officers moved to and fro in the control room below deck, issuing and receiving orders, pulling levers, turning valves, opening vents, and stopping the engines. "Ballast open," one of them reported.

"Is that a good thing?" Jacob asked. He felt a sudden shift in the submarine. He hoped it was not sinking. In a way, it was.

"Dive," Rommond called out.

If there had been anyone left in Dustdelving to witness the Lifemaker's descent, they would have seen the water swiftly displacing, until the massive silver hull, a thousand feet in length, was nowhere to be seen. There was no one there to watch, however, though in time Rommond was certain that there would be, and his old headquarters would be reduced to flames.

Jacob held on tightly to a nearby rail. He thought that they were diving too fast, much to Rommond's amusement. He reassured Jacob that this was a slow descent, that they could drop much quicker, and that when bullets were flying high, it was wise to duck low. Jacob had no problem with ducking, so long as the ground was still below him.

"So are we not using your cosy bridge then?" Jacob asked.

"It's not pressurised," Rommond replied. "But feel free to go up there if you want."

"You know what," Jacob said, "I'll stay down here, if it's all the same."

"A wise man."

Jacob smiled and saluted. "Thank you, sir."

He noticed Taberah resting against the wall near the helm, where she was shown the controls by what looked like a fair-haired and fair-skinned boy. There was not a hint of stubble on him. Jacob thought that maybe Taberah should have been showing the kid the controls instead.

"Who's the lad at the helm?" he asked Rommond.

The nearby crew chuckled and giggled, until Rommond silenced them with a glance. "That," he said sternly, "is the captain of this fine vessel. Nera Alson. And *she* is a very good captain at that. Married to the machinery—even more than I."

Jacob pouted. He looked back over at the captain, but all he could see was the square jaw, the thick eyebrows, and the tight haircut. Of course, a sailor's uniform did not help. There was no figure in it.

"She cuts her hair short to abide by the same rules she demands of her male crew," Rommond explained. "It isn't mandatory, and I told her that we've had lasses in the trenches who don't give themselves a butch cut, but she was adamant about it. She even sleeps on a bunk."

"And you?" Jacob asked.

"I have my own room," Rommond said, "just like you."

Jacob smiled. "I bet it's bigger though."

Rommond stared at him. "It's big enough for your sacred crate of coils."

"Barely."

"Jacob, with the weight of that crate, we could have gotten rid of one of the ballast tanks."

"Happy to help," Jacob said.

"We'd have had to jettison it to surface, however."

"Glad you kept the tanks then."

"Don't get too comfortable, Jacob. There's still plenty left to jettison."

Jacob got the distinct impression the general was not just talking about objects.

Taberah was a fast learner, but there were a bit too many controls in the submarine for her liking. She could barely rest her back against a panel without hitting a switch or twisting a dial. Still, she preferred to ensure she had even a remote understanding of how things were done. She was not exactly comfortable leaving her fate in the hands of others, even if some of them were old friends.

"Do you enjoy this?" Taberah asked.

"Yes," the captain said. "Why wouldn't I?"

"I don't know. It seems a little lonely."

"Sometimes it's just me and the ship."

"And that doesn't bother you?" Taberah wondered.

"No, not really. There's a lot of life beneath the sea."

A moment passed, where Alson only had a conversation with the submarine. She flicked switches and pulled levers, and the ship responded with beeps and flashing lights. Taberah could make out nothing of what it said.

"I never got to see this when I was in the Resistance," Taberah said.

"Rommond likes to keep his cards close to his chest."

Taberah smirked. "He sure does."

"I've been doing test dives for over a year," Alson revealed. "Before that the sub was dry-docked on concrete blocks. Not a drop of water."

"I presume you prefer the water."

"It's why I wanted this job. I live for the sea. I wouldn't have stayed in Rommond's bunkers if it weren't for the promise of seeing the ocean's depths."

"I can't say I share your enthusiasm."

Alson looked up from the controls for a fraction of a second. "This really is the Lifemaker for me. Without it, I might as well be dead. I want to live at sea ... and I want to die at sea."

Taberah knew that where they were going, Alson might just get her wish.

Once things had settled down, and the excess people were ordered to clear the command centre, Jacob found his way to Taberah's room, which was on the deck above his. He was not entirely sure how he got there, as he had wandered up and down many levels, and all the corridors looked pretty much the same. He noticed with some amusement, however, that the higher decks were carpeted, while the lower ones had just bare metal. He wondered if this was a design decision, or if the Lifemaker really was unfinished. The former possibility was discouraging, but the latter one was much more unsettling.

Jacob knocked lightly on Taberah's door, and entered before she could tell him to go away. He found her writing in her diary.

"Writing about me again?" he asked.

"Of course," she said.

"All good, I hope."

"All bad."

"At least I get a mention."

Taberah returned to her journalling. Jacob wondered what she was really writing. *5:45pm*, he mused. *That handsome man Jacob has come to visit again.* Maybe it was more like: *That annoying Jacob has come to bother me again.*

He looked around her quarters as she continued to scribble. It was at least four times the size of his room. Clearly being friends with the general paid dividends in the deeps.

"You've got a nicer room than mine," he said.

"You're lucky you've got your own quarters," Taberah replied. "More than half the crew will be sleeping in bunks."

"Maybe Rommond doesn't want me mixing with his crew."

"Something tells me he'll find you where he shouldn't anyway."

"Female intuition?" Jacob asked.

"Something like that."

Jacob plopped himself down on the single wooden stool and leaned back against the wall.

"Comfy," he said.

"Don't get too comfortable," she replied with a smile. "This isn't your room."

He smiled back, and they locked eyes. If it was a smiling competition, he was winning. If it was a staring contest, she was in the lead.

"I can't say I was very fond of the sea," Taberah remarked, as she continued to hold his gaze. "Too temperamental."

Something you couldn't control, Jacob thought. He felt his gaze waver. "I like the sea," Jacob said. "I just prefer it below me, not above. Living inside it makes me feel—"

"Trapped?"

"You could say that. Every time I look outside those windows and just see water, it feels like I've nowhere to run. Even Blackout wasn't like that."

"Maybe we can get you some curtains," Taberah suggested.

Jacob chuckled. "As long as they aren't floral."

"Maybe ones with fishes on them then."

"Yeah, that'll help."

There was a moment of silence, where Jacob thought he could almost feel a slight dip of the submarine's nose. He waited to see if the stool would slide across the room. Nothing happened.

"You know, I'm sorry," he said at last.

"I didn't know," she replied. "I'm still not sure I do."

"I guess for you words are not enough."

"It depends who speaks them."

Jacob stifled a sigh. "I'm not ready to be a dad," he said. "Hell, I don't think I'll ever be ready."

"You've done fine with Whistler," she pointed out.

"Yeah, well, he's not my kid. And he's a while out of nappies by now."

"I'm not looking for a perfect father," Taberah said. "Whistler's done without one for all his life."

"What happened to his father? Did he die?"

"Are you trying to change the subject?" she asked.

"No … are you?"

"Listen, Jacob. I don't care if you're part of this child's life." She rubbed her hand across her belly. "We'll be fine. What I do want is for you to help the Order and the Resistance to further our goals."

"I'm here, amn't I? It's not like I can help the Regime."

"You can by being in our way."

"Am I in the way?"

"That's your decision, Jacob."

"Well, I'd offer to steer this ship, but submersibles

aren't really my thing. Put this tin can on wheels and I'll drive it across the ocean floor."

"You shouldn't joke," Taberah said. "Rommond's done stranger things with his vehicles before."

Chapter Two

THE STRANGEST LIFE

Much of the first week of the descent was fairly uneventful. While Jacob was mostly thankful for this, a part of him began to yearn for some excitement. A smaller part did not care about the cost.

No one would tell him just how far they had dived, probably, he surmised, to save him the shock of realising just how far he would have to swim to escape his metal cage. He also had another more worrying fear: that they did not actually know how deep they were.

The answer to this riddle did not come from the equipment they had brought. The sounding lines were dropped, but they did not hit the bottom, and did not come up again. Instead the answer came from the wildlife, the fishes and cetaceans that made the various layers of the ocean their home. Like an archaeological dig, the further they went, the stranger the creature, and the easier it was to judge their depth.

But there were parts of the ocean that were not mapped, depths that even Alson had not dived to, and Rommond locked himself in the control room, trying to ensure they did not become the unwitting cartographers of the abyss.

Jacob spent much of his abundant time, when he was not being a general nuisance, staring out at the weird and wonderful sea creatures, nature's own freak show, with free admission.

He found that Whistler was also doing the same from his quarters, and periodically they would frantically call to the other, "Did you see that?" before describing what new water-dwelling wildlife they had seen.

This cheered up Whistler a lot, mostly because it distracted him from his bandages, which protected him from seeing what kind of freak show, in his own eyes, he had become.

As Jacob watched life teeming outside the vessel, he began to wonder if one day he might be sitting there with his own child, watching the fishes. *Maybe it won't be so bad*, he thought, but it was not a thought he held for long.

It took several days to sort out the duty rosters. The crew were put on three rotating shifts, eight hours apart, which meant three rotating dinner hours. Jacob's duty, given directly by Rommond, was to stay out of his way, and out of trouble. For a few months' worth of dinners, Jacob was happy to do nothing.

When Jacob checked the roster and routine sheets, which were pinned at the entrances and exits of each deck, he noted that he had the night shift, which suited him just fine. He also noticed with some amusement that Rommond, Taberah, and Whistler were also on that shift, probably, he presumed, to keep an eye on him.

Another glance at the routine sheet showed that dinner time for the night shift was not universal, but also on rotation, with four half-hour slots in total. Jacob presumed this was because the mess hall was tiny, but on his first visit there he was pleasantly surprised. The room, conveniently close to the main crew quarters, had twelve large tables, and benches on either side of them, all bolted to the floor. It was not lavish, but it was bright and colourful, and it could easily make anyone forget that they were trapped beneath the sea.

"Hell," Jacob said when he entered the mess hall. He stopped near the door to take in the scene. Others with greater hunger squeezed by.

"Don't let Karlsif hear you call it that," Rommond said as he entered the room with Alson, who looked like she had not had a meal all day.

"How big *is* this rust bucket?" Jacob asked.

"Grab a tray and I'll tell you," Rommond said, before loading up his own.

"General," the cook said, giving him a nod. He was known as Karlsif, though no one really knew if that was his first or last name. He made the finest dinner, and prided himself on getting up during each of the submarine's three shifts to make it, leaving breakfast and supper to his assistants. He had a cheerful, rose-tinted face, a balding crown, and an unsteady hand, which resulted in numerous broken plates and other incidents.

Jacob took a bit of everything on offer, and made sure to ladle on plenty of gravy, a luxury he had not had in many years. When he tucked in, it was even more delicious than it looked. He might have tipped the waiter, had he not waited on himself.

"To answer your question," Rommond said, after pushing up his sleeves to avoid them being soiled, "this sub is almost a thousand feet long and two hundred wide. It has five decks, and an ironworks beneath the bottom deck, where we store and work on our other vehicles. It has everything a crew needs, because it was designed with one purpose in mind: to safely house a civilisation beneath the sea, in the event that the Regime conquered land."

"It doesn't have everything," Jacob grumbled. "It doesn't have fresh air."

"We have enough of that stored in tanks," Rommond said. "For a while."

"Until the Regime stops hunting us," Alson added.

Jacob spoke as he munched. "Let's hope they're not as dogged as you lot."

Karlsif hobbled over with a small basket of bread rolls. "Straight from the oven, General."

"Thank you," Rommond said. "Is everything going smoothly?"

Karlsif cast a nervous glance over his shoulder. "It'll be better when I find out who's been stealing food from the pantry."

"It's the salt sea air," Jacob ventured.

"Is that a confession?" Rommond quizzed.

"It's a theory."

"Well, if you and your detective nose find out anything," Karlsif said, "be sure to let me know."

"And me," the general added. "Or we'll need to put the entire crew on rations."

"Does that include you?" Jacob asked.

"Of course. I've survived on worse. But I get a little cranky on rations. So it's better that we find the glutton before then."

Karlsif returned to his duties, glancing now and then across the room, as if he might spot the pantry thief at any moment.

"Now, there's a man who doesn't like the sea," Rommond said, pointing his fork towards the cook. "He's always had a nervous disposition, but he never had the shakes until we boarded this ship."

"You know, the deeper we go," Jacob said, "the more I might join him."

On the sixth day of their journey, the Lifemaker entered an area of the sea where a large sunken city sprawled before and around them.

"Attention all crew and guests of this vessel," Rommond announced over the intercom, "we are passing through the old world now, the old time. Take a moment, please, to remember it, to acknowledge it, to honour it, and to see it in your minds as an example of the very thing we are striving for."

All eyes were fixed on the surroundings, and the Lifemaker drifted slowly through the ruins.

They passed buildings of all sizes, pillars and arches, and even a monumental statue, damaged more by the invasion of the Regime than by the years of erosion.

"This was the old city of Goldwall," Rommond

continued. "Back when gold was more valuable than iron. It was an island city, which only faced threats from pirates, against whom they were well fortified. When the demons came, the people of Goldwall, my people, held them off for weeks, while I fought Domas and his army in the trenches. But our world was exposed to the husk of theirs, and the sands came, and the winds came, until all those beautiful lakes and green pastures were covered or blown south, burying this city in this world's last great sea."

The vessel glided through the remnants, which were vaster than Blackout was. That the once largest city of mankind had become its largest graveyard played heavy on all minds. The chapel of that graveyard, a colossal domed building with many arches, came into view.

"We pass now the dome of the Alda Kalta," the general-turned-tour guide said. "It was once the greatest museum of our world, housing many works of art. It survived the Regime, but it did not survive the flood. Now it still serves its old purpose, for inside those arched walls are many caches of statues and paintings, sealed tight against the eroding waters. That they survive, when so much of our culture did not, gives me hope. That they are locked away by necessity, unable to be seen by our people, makes me angry. These two things I hope you will bring with you, and let them empower you in our fight against the Regime. All of you, all of us, are united aboard the Lifemaker. But around us, in this city that I once called home, there are little lifemakers everywhere."

* * *

On the eighth day of the voyage, Jacob walked in on a meeting between Rommond and some of the senior officers. Taberah and Soasa were also there, and everyone looked at Jacob as he entered.

"Sorry I'm late," he said.

Rommond glowered at him. "You weren't invited."

"I think my invitation is still in the mail."

Taberah looked at Rommond and rolled her eyes. The general turned back to Alson and continued his report.

"We have thirty-four Pure on board," he said, "and they are as precious a cargo to us as anything else we have. I apologise, of course, for speaking of them as a commodity, but the reality is that they are more valuable than anything else we have—even our own lives.

"We made this vessel as a refuge for them, a haven from the Regime, but it has become our own refuge too. Yet we must do everything we can to ensure they survive, for the fate of the human race is in their hands."

"You mean in their loins," Jacob corrected.

"The Regime has submersibles of their own," Rommond continued, raising his voice just a little, "but they can only dive so deep. This gives us a distinct advantage, for if we stay down low, we can avoid detection, and in time they will stop looking for us."

"Our little fireworks display at the Hope factory might motivate them for a bit," Taberah said, and her pride was palpable.

Rommond nodded solemnly. "Thankfully, we built the Lifemaker to last."

The general led the group down to one of the lower decks, where the Pure were gathered. There were no bunks there, but the beds were crammed together. Small children were running around, and babies were crying. Many of the women were near labour, while others looked as though they were not pregnant at all.

Rommond introduced the various people, paying special attention to one of them, a rather thin woman of maybe twenty years, with just the hint of a bump. He brought Taberah to her, as if he thought that she could help.

"This is Marya," he said. He gave Taberah a stern look, as if they had discussed the young expectant mother before, and he expected Taberah to live up to some obligation she had made.

Jacob glanced at Taberah, who seemed more than a little uncomfortable in that room. It did not suit her, but then he thought motherhood did not suit her either. She always looked like she just did not have the time. *The cause* consumed her. Maybe, in time, it would consume him too.

As Taberah spoke with Marya about her pregnancy, never telling her, Jacob noted, about her own, Jacob had a word with the general.

"So, what's with her?" he asked, nodding towards Marya, who was looking everywhere bar at Taberah, and fidgeting excessively, and rattling off a series of *ehs* and *uhms*, as if they were punctuation.

"Some don't take to the idea of motherhood all that well," Rommond said. He paused and looked at Jacob. "Or fatherhood."

Jacob smirked. "I suppose I walked into that one."

They watched Taberah and Marya for another few minutes, noticing their awkward conversation. It seemed that Marya wanted to talk, but could not, whereas Taberah looked more than capable, but much less willing.

"Marya tried to take her life twice," Rommond stated, as if it were like getting out of bed. Perhaps to him, who had taken so many lives, it was.

"That's grim," Jacob said after a pause. "And you talked her out of it?"

"Not me, but others did, eventually."

"Not to sound selfish or anything," Jacob said, "but is it wise bringing someone who's suicidal on board? I mean, what if she tries to sink the ship?"

Rommond chuckled. "Now, now, have a little faith. It would take someone very cunning to send the Lifemaker down."

"So ... that rules out the Resistance then?"

Rommond laughed more heartily. "It rules out you."

"Not to change the subject," Jacob said, "but how long can this thing last down here?"

Rommond smiled. "You mean, how long can *we* last?"

"Well, that's a different question."

"If well-stocked, this *thing* can stay submerged for six months."

"Hell," Jacob blurted.

"At our depths, dear chap, we'll be close enough."

"I'm just glad it isn't nine months."

"I take it you don't want to be trapped here when the baby is born."

Jacob looked again at Taberah. "More like I don't want my kid to be born in this rickety tin can."

"As it stands, Jacob, this *tin can* might be the safest place to give birth."

Jacob surveyed the Pure, the fate of humanity crammed together like sardines. "Or the only place," he said.

Chapter Three

THE DEVILS OF THE DEEP

On the ninth day of their journey, the sea stopped being calm.

Jacob sat with his face against the glass of the small window in his cabin, steaming it up with his breath. He had not seen anything for over an hour but weeds and silt.

"Still nothing," he heard Whistler call from the other room. They had made a chart of all the creatures they had spotted so far, which Whistler wanted to present to the captain. There were many empty spaces, and Jacob hoped to see anything to help him pass the time.

Suddenly something lashed at the window, and Jacob cried out and flinched. Then it was gone, and Jacob could barely control his racing heart and fleeting breath. He pressed his face against the pane and tried to peer to either side, to see if something was clinging to the hull. There was nothing there but the flora of the sea.

He heard another crash, but further off. Whistler raced in, his eyes wide with wonder and terror. "I saw something," he stammered.

"So did I."

Ten minutes passed, and while their hearts slowed and their breathing returned to normal, their eyes remained alert. Whistler would not return to his room now. He insisted that he would get a better view from Jacob's window, and an even better one from behind Jacob's shoulder.

"It was like," Whistler began, clutching Jacob's arm. "I don't know. I didn't get a proper look."

Jacob turned and shushed him. He heard a series of raps against the hull. They were distant, but something told him that they were not the only witnesses of this fleeting ocean beast. He got up quickly and headed into the corridors.

"Wait for me!" Whistler cried, and ran after him.

They knocked on cabin doors, asking if anyone had seen or heard anything. Most had not, but a few thought something had grazed the ship. None of them seemed worried. They said that it was a common occurrence, and would become more common the further down they went.

For Jacob, however, it was just the excitement he needed. He wanted to know exactly what it was, and what it could do to the submarine. Whistler did not seem as keen on adding this particular creature to his chart.

They encountered Soasa in the corridors. She looked as though she had just seen something too, and might have been heading for her box of dynamite.

"Not another corridor dance," Soasa grumbled. "Go back the way you came."

"But I think it went that way, towards the stern."

"You saw it?" Soasa asked.

"Just a glance," Jacob said. "I want to know what it is."

Suddenly the submarine shook violently, turning slightly on its side. Anyone in the corridors fell against the walls, while anyone in the rooms fell against the windows or doors.

"Come on!" Jacob called, and he raced towards the back of the ship, with Whistler and Soasa following swiftly behind him. They no longer knocked on doors, but made straight for the stern, where a much larger window would give them a greater view of whatever was out there.

They arrived, and the window was bigger than Jacob expected. It was reinforced with metal, which made it look a little like a spider's web. *Something tells me this is too big a fly.*

"I don't see anything," Whistler said as he hung back near the corridor. He tapped his heel up and down, as if her was preparing for a race—or preparing to flee.

Suddenly something came straight for the glass. A giant whale struck against the hull, lashing it with its tail. It turned full circle and charged again, ramming the ship and rocking the crew inside. Then another joined it, and the two crashed into the submarine like torpedoes. Jacob thought that the glass might crack or break, but it held. The question was: for how long?

"They're going to wreck the ship," Soasa said.

"Maybe you can blow them up," Jacob suggested.

"Sure," Soasa replied. "Because fuses light real well under water."

"Yours lights just fine."

"Maybe we should tell Rommond," Whistler said. He was already several steps into the corridor, bracing himself against the walls.

Jacob smiled. "I have a feeling he already knows."

When Jacob and the others hurried into the control room, they found that everyone was in a fluster. What few officers were not glued to their seats were thrown to the floor every time they tried to race from station to station.

"Get him out of here," Rommond said when he spotted the smuggler. "We're busy enough as it is."

"Just reporting for harpoon duty," Jacob said.

Rommond dismissed him with the wave of his hand, before returning his focus to the control panels on either side of Alson. He and Taberah ran from side to side, adjusting switches, releasing pressure from the valves, and filling one of the tanks with water. The nose of the submarine began to dip. Jacob clutched a set of pipes, hoping for dear life that they would not come loose.

Then the ship rocked again, and they felt as though they were being lifted up.

"There must be one beneath us," Alson said.

"It doesn't matter," Rommond replied. "We need to dive."

He pulled the rope that sounded the dive alarm. *A little late*, Jacob thought, as the submarine dipped again, and he clutched the pipes more tightly. He saw Soasa and Whistler grabbing the door frame.

"We're going down too steep, too fast," Alson said. Her boots were firmly pressed against the panel in front of her. It was lucky her seat was bolted to the floor.

Several more whales bashed against the hull, knocking it from side to side, as if it were on a rocky sea. To the whales, those movements were tiny. To everyone inside the Lifemaker, they were like earthquakes.

"We're not going fast enough," Rommond said, before opening another valve. The ship sank even further, head first, and the propeller kicked into overdrive. *The only way to dive*, Jacob thought.

As they clung to anything they could, and as the submarine descended into darker waters at incredible speeds, Alson flicked on the searchlights at the front of the vessel. The sea lit up ahead of them, and from the control room window they could see angry whales skimming back and forth.

"Maybe this will scare them off," she said.

For some it did, but for others the lights only made them angrier, and while they avoided the glare, they rammed the back of the submarine, dinting the hull. The light also revealed something else: dozens of smaller whales, flitting about the waters in a frenzy.

"This must be their nursing ground," Alson noted. "No wonder they're angry."

"They think we're invaders," Rommond pointed out.

"In a way, we are," Jacob said.

"How do we make them see that we mean them no harm?" Taberah asked.

"We can't exactly send a message in a bottle," Jacob said.

"We get out of their territory as quickly as possible," Rommond said.

They continued to dive, and the whales continued to strike the submarine, though their attacks became less frequent, until finally they did not come at all. Fifteen minutes passed, then half an hour, and then Rommond and Alson straightened up the ship and decreased the speed.

"There," Rommond said. "We're at a lower depth. We shouldn't see any more of them."

"Maybe not," Jacob remarked, "but what if we see something worse?"

Chapter Four

THE COPPER VIXENS

Jacob walked Taberah back to her quarters after the incident with the whales, which she initially protested about.

"I don't need a chaperone," she told him.

Jacob grinned. "Maybe I do."

For several nights he met her coming from the command room, and told her how he trembled, and begged her to walk him home. She slapped him on the shoulder, and told him he was not funny, and insisted she had better things to do, and tried to find another route away from him–but in time she walked with him the iron roads and steel laneways of the ship, the oil lamps their moonlight.

"You don't seem that happy here," Jacob noticed. He had meant to say it many times, but he thought it might be due to the lack of sunlight, or the stress of work, or perhaps even his company.

"If you think you're trapped here," Taberah replied, "then you have no idea."

"Aren't these all friends?"

"Some of them, yes."

* * *

On one of their nightly walks, they took a longer route—the scenic route, some might have called it, were it not for the fact that it brought them down several decks, close to the sealed-off ironworks, where the gaslights grew dimmer, and the people grew more dour-faced, and dour of mood. These bleak areas, in some ways the slums of the ship, were not the safest territory to traverse, and all kinds of clowns were out, with not a smile among them.

The ringleader of that iron circus, Ana Alakovi, made sure to block Taberah and Jacob. She did not need to do much, for she was tall and broad, muscled to the teeth. She looked as though she had built herself, bit by bit, banging everything into shape, riveting it all together, soldering it all in place. She made sure to show her bulky arms through a tank top, and if she was not already tall enough, her multi-coloured hair towered above her in an almost perfect rectangle. She also had bolts and cogs in her ears and nose, and probably also her tongue. Maybe there was no part of her that had not been at one point or other hammered or pierced or clamped.

"If it isn't the devil herself," Alakovi said. She looked down her nose at Taberah and folded her arms, which made the muscles bulge even more.

"Who's that?" Jacob whispered to Taberah. He wished he had not.

"You don't be talkin' about me as if I'm not in the room," Alakovi boomed. "If you're with her, you're likely just as bad as her."

"Maybe worse," Jacob tried, again wishing he had not spoken at all. It seemed that Whistler was not the only one with a loose tongue.

"A perfect match then," Alakovi hissed. "The devil found another devil. You's can rot in Hell together."

"If this is Hell," Jacob said, "you'll be rotting here with us."

"Oh, I'll knock you back to before the Harvest, boy!" Alakovi growled, and she had to be held back by many of the other women. It took half a dozen to stop her advancing a single pace. She turned her attention back to Taberah when she could not get her fists on Jacob.

"Sorry, miss," Jacob said, "but I really don't know who you are."

"You don't know who *I* am?" she bawled, bashing her fists against her chest. "I'm the Copper Matron, is who I am. These are my sisters, sisters of blood and sisters of spirit, and together we're the Copper Vixens. And that wench o' yours—yeah, we all know *your* type—used to be one o' us."

She turned again to Taberah. "Should've known you'd be no good, you and your amulets 'stead of a good ol' pair o' pliers. You worked your magic on us once before, but no more! We're wise to you now, girl. We got the knowledge o' you. You've got some nerve comin' back here after what you did!"

"What did you do?" Jacob whispered to Taberah.

He should have known that Alakovi would respond instead. "She went and stabbed Rommond in the back, is what she did. And she's probably still got the knife!"

"I didn't stab him in the back," Taberah protested, and while her defence was strong, in the face of

Alakovi's volcanic temper, it seemed weak.

"What do you call an attempted coup then?"

"We wanted different things for the Resistance."

"No. You wanted the same thing: *control*. Only Rommond had it and you didn't. And he earned it. You tried to steal it like the backstabbin' thief you are."

"Let's go," Taberah said to Jacob, turning away from the battle.

"Oh, you want to leave now, do you? You don't get your way, so you bolt and run. Just like you did the first time. Just like you'll always do. You ain't got no stayin' power, no stamina, girl. And you *damn* well got no loyalty. No wonder so few went with you."

There was a chorus of *uhm-hmms* from the Vixens behind and around her, many of whom mimicked her pose, folding their arms and raising their eyebrows. Many of them had more muscles than Jacob did, and they looked like they knew how to fix anything. *That'll come in handy*, Jacob thought. *I know how to break things.*

Jacob was surprised to see Taberah taking so much abuse from this woman without fighting back. Instead, she seemed to be fighting back her own responses, and perhaps that was wise, because the Copper Vixens did not look like they would hold back the Matron forever.

"I tried to work something out," Taberah said. "I tried to get Rommond to listen to my ideas, but they didn't figure in his master plan, and he's not really a man of change. We went our separate ways, and I think the Resistance is stronger for it."

"Yeah right," Alakovi said. "Your Order would've

never existed were it not for Rommond. He listened to you all the time. Sure didn't he listen to you more than he listened to rest o' us? That's why your betrayal stings so bad. You were the scorpion we trusted."

"I don't have to listen to this," Taberah said, as she walked away.

"You know who I pity?" Alakovi roared at her. "The boy."

Taberah turned to charge at her, but Jacob held her back. Taberah might have had the fire, but Alakovi had the muscle. "You're not the only matron around here," Taberah screamed at her. It took a dozen of the Vixens to hold the Copper Matron back. They were like two bulls, and none of them would give in.

"Let her loose, boy," Alakovi said. "The scorpion's power is in surprise. Oh, I'm not surprised any more. I'll squash her like the bug she is!"

Jacob hauled Taberah away, and the Vixens kept Alakovi pegged to the spot. The Copper Matron shouted after them, pummelling them with her words.

"And you can tell your girls, Taberah—*all of 'em*—that I better not see 'em near the Vixens or I'll make sure they need a copper plate to replace their skulls!"

In time Jacob managed to pull Taberah out of sight and earshot of the Copper Vixens, which helped to calm her down. They sat on the steps leading up to the next deck, and Taberah held her head and stared at the ground.

"I can't blame her," she said.

"I can."

"The thing that I don't get though, is why Rommond doesn't feel as betrayed."

"Maybe you're just part of his master plan."

Taberah humphed. "More like the other way 'round. The Copper Matron is right about a lot of things. The Order wouldn't have existed if it weren't for Rommond and his toys. We'd have never gotten the *Glass* for the amulets."

"You mean that mystical crystal stuff?"

"Yeah. I discovered it, but Rommond helped me get it from the mines. The Glassfinder Project. Our first big win against the Regime."

"And let's not forget," Jacob said, "that it got me a job."

"Well, you can thank Rommond for that as well," Taberah replied. "That's one thing Rommond and I always had in common. We always look for the bigger picture. Maybe that's why he doesn't hate me for trying to take control."

"Only because he won."

"I'm not so sure he did."

"It doesn't exactly look like you won either," Jacob noted.

"No," she said with a sigh. "I think we both lost."

"Well, that's all in the past now, right?"

"Kind of. It doesn't help that the Copper Matron doesn't forgive. She has this whole sorority, with oaths and codes of conduct. Once you're out, you're out for good."

"I guess I didn't make a good first impression then."

"Showing up with me was all it took."

"Then it was worth it."

"Thanks," Taberah said.

"For what?"

"For holding me back."

"Hey, I'll hold you any day," he said with a wink.

She smiled. "I didn't exactly feel like getting beaten up today."

"Can't be good for the baby."

"The Copper Matron doesn't know about that, or she wouldn't hit me."

"I'm just glad I didn't challenge her to an arm wrestle," Jacob said.

"And me?" Taberah asked.

"I wouldn't challenge a woman with child."

"Afraid you'd lose?"

"Yeah," Jacob said. "There's a strong little boy in there after all."

"Or a stronger girl."

Jacob nodded. "If the Copper Vixens are what girls are like on board the Lifemaker, then she'll do just fine."

Chapter Five

A GAME OF WITS

The submarine descended into a deeper and darker part of the ocean, and perhaps there were fishes there, but Jacob and Whistler could no longer see them. In any case, Jacob had grown bored of that game, so he resumed his other pastime of wandering about the decks, looking for something to do, or someone to bother.

Soasa kept out of his way, or perhaps he kept out of hers, and Taberah locked herself away with Alson, discussing the journey ahead. It seemed to Jacob that she was trying to learn how to steer the ship, and that it was more than just mere curiosity. Perhaps she did not trust Alson's abilities, though she seemed capable enough, or maybe Taberah would just rather be in charge. It was also possible that she was simply avoiding Jacob, a scenario which Jacob frequently thought, and frequently discarded.

He entertained the idea of popping by the Copper Vixens and offering his best estimation of the secret handshake. He dismissed the thought when he considered the not-so-secret black eye he would likely walk away with.

He bumped into Doctor Mudro, who had just

come from Whistler's quarters. The doctor had an unusual gait, as if he was trying to hide a limp; his sleight of hand might have been good, but the same could not be said for his sleight of foot. He hobbled down the corridor to Jacob, puffing on his pipe, which was tightly packed with the pain-killing leaf. The smoke trailed behind him like breadcrumbs.

"Should you be smoking in here?" Jacob asked. "Low oxygen and all."

"It's perfectly safe," Mudro muttered through his pipe.

"Is it for your leg?" Jacob asked.

"It's for my mind," the doctor replied. "Clears the head."

"Funny, that. Smoke seems to dull everything else."

"You could call it magic," the doctor said, drawing out the words as if they were a special incantation. Perhaps to one who smoked the leaf, they were.

Mudro might have limped, but he had a hurried pace, as if he was always rushing from one patient to another. Jacob found that he was almost skipping to keep up. He fancied the pair made a humorous sight.

"How did you get into it?" Jacob asked as they went.

"Hmm?"

"The magic tricks and all."

"*Tricks* is such a crude word," the doctor grumbled. "What you do getting those amulets into Blackout is a trick."

"More like sweat and hard work." *And a whole lot of skill*, he thought.

"Magic is not about illusion," Mudro explained, stopping suddenly to wave his hand before Jacob's face; Jacob could not help but follow it. "It's about showing you a different world."

I'm sure the leaf does enough of that, Jacob thought.

The doctor started off again, half-limping, half-galloping. Jacob wondered if he was intending to disappear.

"So how did you get into it?" Jacob asked again. "It's an interesting pastime."

Mudro halted once more, and Jacob almost passed him by. The wave of the doctor's hand was more aggressive now. "I was a magician before I was a doctor. *Medicine* is my pastime."

How reassuring, Jacob thought. *I wonder if you put that on your resume.*

"How about a magic show?" Jacob proposed. It certainly beat sitting around waiting for something to happen. Though finding a rabbit within the tightly-sealed walls of the Lifemaker might have been more a miracle.

"Another time," the doctor replied. "I'll be handling a different deck of cards tonight."

"Oh?"

"Poker at the general's quarters."

"Maybe I'll join you."

Mudro raised an index finger to Jacob's face, as if he were about to cast a spell. "You mean," he said, with a showman's smile, "maybe I'll smuggle you in."

Jacob grinned. "Well, you can always learn a new trick."

* * *

They arrived at the general's dimly-lit quarters, where a group of men huddled around the small square table to worship the sacred god of gambling. Rommond was not amused when Jacob emerged from behind Mudro, like the disappearing man who has been made reappear. Rommond would have preferred that the magic act ended at the first half.

"Deal me in," Jacob said, grabbing one of the empty chairs and sitting down in a lounging manner, as if these were his quarters.

"This is a crew's game," Rommond replied.

"The doctor's not part of your crew," Jacob pointed out. "He's one of Taberah's people."

"He was one of mine first," the general said coolly.

Mudro pretended he had not heard a thing. He hid himself in the smoke of the leaf.

It was not yet time to offer his hand, so Jacob offered a grin. "Consider me a new recruit then."

"New recruits usually clean the boilers," Lieutenant Tradam said. He sat on the general's right. An empty chair was on his left.

"And clean out the crew when playing cards," Jacob responded.

Rommond eyed him carefully. Jacob was hoping a not-so-subtle challenge would work. He got the distinct impression that Rommond knew this, but he also got the impression that it was working.

"No one plays for free," the general said. "It's one coil buy-in."

"You don't dabble," Jacob said, and he flicked a coil onto the table. "I've got a few to spare." He rattled his pocket, which he thought might rattle Rommond's wits. The general stared back nonchalantly.

"You might find, Jacob," Rommond said, "that money is less useful beneath the sea."

He began dealing the cards around the table, pausing ever so slightly as his hands passed by the empty chair. Jacob was focused more on the cards themselves, and on the good hand he had been dealt.

"Fold," a younger man of about twenty, sitting to the left of the empty chair said. He slapped his cards down on the table in defeat.

"It's the first round," Rommond said. "Don't give up so easily."

"I've got nothing," the lad protested.

"It's better to have the bad hand at the beginning than at the end," the general said, and his voice became suddenly more severe. "I don't expect any of my men to surrender in the first battle ... or the last."

The young man took back up his cards. There was silence in the room, punctuated by Mudro's periodic puffs.

"So, where's the ladies?" Jacob asked.

"Most are having a meeting."

"Copper Vixens?"

Rommond nodded.

"So does that make this our fraternity?" Jacob wondered.

"In a way."

"What's the password then?"

Rommond smiled. "Only *members* know."

"Join the club," Tradam said, passing a bottle of whiskey to Jacob. "Get some neck oil down you."

They continued to play, dropping cards and

raising bets. By the second round, Jacob had already thrown in three coils. For an average worker, if they were not working for the Regime for free, that was three months' wages.

"This is daylight robbery," Jacob said. "Do you not use halves and quarters?"

"Why have half when you can have the whole coil?" Rommond replied.

"This is one of his tactics," Mudro said, waving his hand over his cards, as if changing their suits and numbers. "He gets us up here on the pretence of a game, and he empties our pockets to further aid the war effort. Sleight of hand if ever I saw it."

Rommond smirked and titled his hat to the doctor.

Jacob noticed that Rommond straightened up the deck between every play, even if it was only mildly skewed. Jacob took some delight in slapping his cards down in as haphazard a fashion as he could manage. Rommond pretended it did not bother him, but it clearly did.

"I guess you like to keep the deck as straight as your uniform," Jacob said.

"A messy uniform shows a messy mind," Rommond replied. "Show the enemy none of your mind, or better yet, show them what you want them to see."

"So you're a bluffing man."

"Best way to play," the doctor interjected. Jacob hoped he was not bluffing when he told people they were healed. He found himself thinking about Whistler, sitting alone with his scars. He tried to redirect his focus to his cards.

Despite years of gambling experience, more often than not to pay off debts rather than to play for fun, Jacob found that neither luck nor skill were on his side. Rommond played every hand with a straight face, and he was almost impossible to read. It was no surprise that he ended up winning most of the rounds.

"So the sharks are not just outside," Jacob observed, as he watched, with a hint of horror, his hard-earned coils leaving his side of the table.

"If I am a shark," Rommond said, biting the edge of one of the coils, as if to show his jaws, "then what does that make you?"

The other players cheered at this remark, and Mudro banged his fists on the table, as if drumming up a beat to a showdown.

"A little fish, I guess," Jacob said. "With a lot of coils." He placed down another stack of the currency, face down, where the Iron Emperor's iron gaze could not be seen. It always seemed like that hallowed leader was watching everything. In a way, he was.

"Who needs the Treasury," Mudro said, "when we've got Jacob here?"

By the end of the night, Jacob had been bled dry. Mudro, a more cautious player, still had a single coil, which he rotated between his fingers, and Tradam had exactly what he started with, having lost and regained his bets. Rommond, however, was the undisputed winner, with several neatly stacked towers of coils on his side of the table. If it had been Jacob, they would have made a single, glorious pile.

"A final game," the general announced.

Jacob did not want to be left out at the end, so he emptied his pockets, casting everything, lint and all, on the table. Rommond bit his lip as he looked at the mess before him.

"There's a coil in there somewhere," Jacob said. He began to rummage through.

"Stop," Rommond said, and he reached over to pull out the card that Cala had given to the smuggler. "What's this?"

"Oh, just a friend's details."

"Tell me about this friend."

"Just an old girlfriend. Nothing serious. Why?"

"Because this emblem here, the fist on the cloud, belongs to a splinter group of the Resistance, and they've been a splinter in my side ever since. They're a dangerous group called the Armageddon Brigade."

"Well, she isn't exactly a *group* kind of person."

"They're a very loose-knit group, Jacob. They could have called themselves Chaos."

"Well, that sounds more her cup of tea."

"Why do have her card?"

"Because she gave it to me, and I tend not to throw things away."

"Have you contacted her?" Rommond grilled.

"No."

"Has she contacted you?"

"Not exactly."

"Not exactly?"

"Well, we bumped into each other in Blackout when I was smuggling out Taberah's loot."

"Did she ask you to sign up to any missions?"

"No."

"Are you certain?"

"I think I'd know," Jacob said. "Then again, I wasn't entirely sure I had signed up to join the Resistance either."

"When we get back to the surface, I strongly recommend you avoid her if she's associating with this group."

"Oh, don't worry," Jacob said. "I had every intention of avoiding her anyway."

Rommond watched him for a moment before dealing the final round, and he continued to watch him as each card was placed down. Perhaps he was wondering if Jacob was an infiltrator from the Armageddon Brigade. *As if I need another reason for you to hate me*, Jacob thought.

Before the players took their cards, Jacob tried to change the subject.

"What's with the empty chair?" he asked. "Were we expecting someone else?"

There was a sudden intense silence, where awkward glances were exchanged with everyone bar Rommond himself. It took a moment for the general to respond.

"That is for Brooklyn."

"Okay, you've *got* to tell me. Who is Brooklyn? I presume it's a who."

Another awkward moment. "If you win this game," Rommond said, "I'll tell you."

Perhaps it was Fate that governed that game, but Jacob found the cards were stacked in his favour. The problem with Fate is that it usually conspired against him, so he saw no reason why it should help him now. He wondered if Rommond, master of strategy, secretly wanted to talk to someone, to open up, when this desert world had closed him down.

Whatever Rommond's secret desires might have been, he played as tactically as ever, keeping Jacob on his toes for the entire game. Jacob enjoyed the challenge, and he enjoyed even more when he won.

"That's enough for tonight," Rommond said. "But who fancies a night cap?"

"I'll hang back for another," Jacob volunteered; it beat volunteering for the Resistance. "A long night deserves a lot of night caps."

"I think the rest of us should be getting back to work," Tradam said, "or bed. We're not all night owls like you two."

Mudro disappeared, leaving behind a trail of smoke, and Tradam led the others out, closing the door behind him. Rommond tidied up the table, clearing away the glasses, which he put in a cabinet that had circular cut-outs for them, so they could not fall and smash in a dive or surface manoeuvre.

Once Rommond had tidied up, he turned up one of the gas lamps, giving Jacob a better view of the room, which he had barely paid any attention to when there was a chance of winning money on the table. The room was decorated with the contents of the general's bunker, including the mysterious plaque bearing the name Brooklyn, which had a central spot, as if it were an idol. *Some kind of god?* Jacob wondered. *Let's hope the worship pays off.*

The room was markedly different to Rommond's

bunker, however, because it did not have walls so much as it had bookshelves, and the paintings were placed over these, and sometimes behind these, and the bookcases were chained to the walls, and some of the books were chained to the bookcases.

"All alphabetical, I presume," Jacob said.

Rommond smiled and handed the smuggler a glass of sherry. "Of course."

"Can't say I'm much of a reader. I tend to cut holes in them to store amulets."

"I'm glad you've found a new vocation then," Rommond said. "I rather like my books, like I presume you rather like your hands."

Jacob laughed. "Don't worry. I won't be cutting up your books any time soon."

"Or any time at all," the general said.

"I'm too busy working for you lot. Different job, but same master, it seems."

"Really? I don't remember ever employing you."

"You take who you can."

"That's Tabs' methodology, not mine."

"Then you put up with whoever Taberah takes," Jacob said with a grin.

"Indeed."

"So then," Jacob said after a brief pause. "Pay up. Tell me who Brooklyn is."

Rommond strolled over to one of the bookcases and stared for a moment at the volumes, as if he was looking for some secret switch that would reveal the secret of who Brooklyn was. Then he took a black and white photograph from his inside pocket, perfectly preserved in a clear film coating, with not a fold or bend in the card. He showed it to Jacob, but would not let him touch it. It depicted a man in his late thirties, with a clean-shaven face, and long, dark hair that went past his shoulders. He had unusually large eyes, and though there was no colour in the photograph, his complexion was dark. Jacob thought that he looked like a member of one of the warring tribes in central Altadas, many of whom had turned their spears on the Regime in recent years.

"He is—*was*—" Rommond paused. "He is everything to me. The Regime captured him three years ago, and we, the Resistance as a whole, have suffered ever since. Most of our machines, our landships, the Lifemaker itself, were designed by him. He had an affinity with machinery that no other could match. He said he was in communion with the spirits that govern contraptions of all kinds, and at first I did not believe him, until I saw what he could create."

By now Rommond was holding the photograph in both hands gently, as if remembering what it was like to hold Brooklyn in his arms. He stared at the picture as he talked.

"They tried to ransom him, but the price was our surrender. I couldn't surrender. How could one life, one love, be saved at the expense of the lives of everyone else? How many loves would then be lost? I … I couldn't surrender."

The general fell into silence, and Jacob had no words good enough to break it. Instead, he broke the emptiness with his presence, and he stood there, facing the general, until it seemed that Rommond would rather be alone. As Jacob left the room, and felt for the first time some sympathy for the general, who looked as though he was holding himself together with his uniform, Rommond called back to him.

"Now you know," he said. "Originally it wasn't personal, this war of ours. I'm trying to stop it from becoming personal. Maybe that's another game I am not winning. But now you know why my hatred of the demons is so strong. When they took him from me, they took everything. I want to make sure they know how that feels."

Chapter Six

THE GOOD NEWS

Jacob noticed that Whistler often spent more time in his room than in his own, even though they were virtually identical. The boy had a habit of bumping into the crate of coils every time he entered the room, as if to suggest there was not room enough aboard for it. This irritated Jacob more than he thought it should. It bothered him more that it was Whistler who was making these passive aggressive condemnations.

"There was space enough for that crate before you came in," Jacob said after one of these incidences.

Whistler pouted. "Why do you even keep it?" he asked.

"You've got to be joking, right?"

"No."

"It's money, kid. You don't throw away money."

"Taberah used to say that Rommond throws away money all the time, on stuff he doesn't use."

"You mean all his war toys? I'm kind of glad he spent big on this tin can."

"Why don't you give him the coils?" Whistler asked.

"I already gave him plenty last night."

"What do you mean?"

"Gambl—never mind. I'm probably a bad enough influence on you already."

"No, you're not."

"Your mother might disagree."

"Well, why did she let you stay then?"

"To babysit you."

Whistler cocked his head. "I don't need baby-sitting."

"No, kid, you don't." *At your age*, Jacob thought, *I was working. I suppose, in a way, you are too. Slaving away for 'the cause'.*

Whistler stood with his arms folded in defiance. He replaced his usual slouch with a puffed chest and arched back. Perhaps he thought he looked like more of a man. That he was barely five feet tall, and thin and weak, with not a whisker on his chin, somewhat ruined the illusion he was going for.

Jacob could not help but smile. "So, speaking of babysitting—"

"I usually look after myself."

"All right! I was just kidding."

"I'm on my way to being a man."

"Look, kid. Sit down."

Whistler reluctantly sat down, as if doing it any quicker would somehow prove he was still a child, being told what to do.

"I just wanted you to know," Jacob continued, "that, with all that's going on with your mother, it can be a bit scary and all, but it'll all work out in the end."

"What do you mean?"

"With the baby."

"What baby?"

"Hell … did you not know? Did she not tell you?"

Whistler's blank expression said more than words could. Jacob was not sure how to respond. Maybe Taberah was working up the courage to tell him. Perhaps she had a plan, and Jacob was spoiling the surprise, or that moment of bonding between them. He debated whether or not he should change the topic, brush it off as a misinterpretation, or a joke. In the end, however, he knew that Whistler was too smart to fall for that.

"She's having a baby. We're having a baby. Me and her." The words sounded strange to him. Surreal. A year ago the concept of having a child was alien to him. In many ways, it still was.

There was an awkward, intense moment of silence, where the news was germinating in Whistler's mind, and the possibility of Whistler not liking it was festering in Jacob's. Maybe that was why Taberah had not told him. Maybe she feared his reaction. Yet it did not seem like her to fear anything at all.

"A little brother?" Whistler asked in time.

"Or sister, as Taberah keeps insisting."

Whistler smiled the broadest smile, and Jacob could not help but follow suit.

"I get to have a little brother or sister!" Whistler said, and he followed it with a cheer. He stood up and wandered around the room, as if practising a demonstration to the newborn on how to walk.

Jacob was relieved. He was expecting Whistler to be hurt.

"Are you not upset that she didn't tell you?"

Whistler halted and sat back down. His excitement abated, like a fire beneath a sudden rain. "She doesn't really tell me things," he said.

"Even big things like this?"

"*Especially* big things like this. It's probably because I blab so much. I'm a," and he paused for a moment where it seemed he was racking his brain for a word he had heard before, "liability."

"You're not a liability," Jacob said. "Hell, if anything, *I'm* the liability."

"Maybe that's why we get on," Whistler suggested.

Jacob chuckled. "We must form a union. Liabilities unite!" He raised his hand for a high-five, which Whistler performed in a sloppy manner, as if he had never done it before.

"She'll want a girl," Whistler said.

"I think most women do."

"Not because of that. Because a girl will be Pure too, and can continue our species. It doesn't matter with the boys. We're useless."

"The girls might say that," Jacob said, "but they still need us if they want to have a baby."

"I think Taberah wished I was a girl. Then I could help the human race."

"I'm sure she's happy with you as you are. And you *are* helping. I mean, who else is keeping watch for the demons in our ranks?" He regretted this last comment immediately, because it seemed to unsettle Whistler. That he had failed to blow the whistle on Teller likely played upon his mind.

"I guess," the boy said in time.

"You know, for someone who supposedly can't keep a secret, you kept the fact that Taberah's one of the Pure closely guarded."

"It wasn't easy. I wanted to tell everyone. It's good to know that the Pure are real, that we won't all die out. People need a little hope."

"So long as it's not the drug," Jacob said with a chuckle. "I think, in this world, people have had enough of that."

Jacob had barely finished his sentence when he thought he saw the shadow of a figure in the room. He turned quickly, but it was gone. It left darker shadows in his mind.

"What is it?" Whistler asked.

"Nothing," Jacob said after a tense pause. "Probably just a ghost."

"Don't say that."

"Better a ghost than a demon."

Yet something told Jacob that it was not nothing, and that it was not a ghost or demon. That it might be human should have brought relief to his mind, but he found it strangely more unsettling.

Chapter Seven

THE MINE FIELD

For those who do not want to be found, the black depths of the ocean are a perfect refuge. Yet the blindness is shared among friend and foe, and uncharted waters are a dangerous place to be wandering blind. For several days the Lifemaker was relying on sonar only, but this was a new technology, and for many of those on board, sound was not as strong as sight.

Suddenly the submarine shook violently, throwing people from their posts. Jacob struggled to his feet only to end up on the floor again as the ship trembled beneath the waves.

"Don't tell me we've found a bigger whale," he cried as he clambered up.

But it was not a creature of nature, difficult to reason with, but rather a creation of machinery, impossible to reason with. In the black waters where the Lifemaker was invisible, there were hundreds more invisible contraptions: mines.

"All stop," Rommond ordered. Alson turned the engines off. The propeller stopped spinning, and the submarine ground to a halt, only inches away from another floating mine.

A man raced up from the lower levels. "We have a leak," he said. "A big one."

"Can Boulder fix it?"

"He's on it right now. God, he's half-submerged! But he'll fix it, providing we don't ram another mine."

"We won't," Rommond promised. Alson did not look as confident.

"I know we want to conserve energy, Rommond," Taberah said, "but I think we should go all out on this."

Rommond nodded. "Lights, full flood."

The lights of the submarine bored through the darkness of the deep, revealing what appeared to be an endless field of mines ahead. All of them were black, and would have been virtually invisible were it not for the Lifemaker's powerful lights, which consumed so much energy that they made the few electrical interior lights flicker. Many were glad then that they relied on oil-lamps, gaslights, and candles instead.

"Why didn't we pick these up on sonar?" Rommond asked. He was calm when he was angry, and the difference might not have been noticeable at all were it not for a slight change in pitch in his voice. Jacob noticed that change now.

Alson was flustered; the mines attacked her ability as a captain as much as they attacked the hull of the ship. "They seem to be masked somehow."

Rommond's eyes betrayed his worry. "If they can mask mines, perhaps they can mask a submarine as well."

"They don't need submarines," Jacob said.

"Enough of these and this'll be the Deathmaker."

"Did they drop all these now, or were they here before?" Rommond asked.

"I don't know," Alson said. "We never came this far east before."

"Does it matter?" Jacob asked.

"It matters because the former suggests they have an idea where we are. I'd rather they just mined off their territory before we took to the sea."

"I'm inclined to think they did this a while back," Alson postulated. "Some of the mines are rusty. And besides, there are too many of them to drop overnight."

"Don't underestimate them," Rommond said. "There are a lot of demons to do the dropping." He paused to survey the underwater wall ahead of them. "Can we go around?"

"It looks like they cover a vast territory."

"Find a way," Rommond ordered.

Alson and Taberah began to immediately map the mines, though they bobbed up and down a little, and some drifted slightly, possibly from the shifting waters that the Lifemaker had caused when it was in motion. Hours passed, and Alson guided the submarine along the edge of the underwater minefield, while Taberah carefully noted down everything they found.

In time, they reported their findings to Rommond.

"We can't go around," Taberah said, "but we can go through."

Jacob thought it was just like her to suggest swimming through a minefield.

"How?" Rommond asked.

"There are small gaps between the mines, and we've plotted a course for a hundred leagues. We may need to nudge one or two mines out of the way, but otherwise it should all be down to dexterity."

"Well, Alson is the most dexterous captain I know," Rommond said. "What about diving or rising? Can we avoid the mines altogether?"

"It doesn't look like it," Alson said. "It seems that the Regime weighted mines differently so that they would ward off intruders at any level of the sea. Of course, we can try searching deeper, but there are some depths I haven't been before, so those are untested waters, so to speak."

"Exploration can wait," Rommond said. "I'd rather not take too many risks with the Pure on board."

"Why don't we just sit here on this side of the mines?" Jacob asked. "Do we really have to move at all?"

"It's unwise to stay in the same place for too long," Rommond explained. "There is a greater chance of getting caught."

"And there's an even greater chance of us getting blown up if we skip through a minefield."

"We are going east," Rommond stated.

"Why?"

"Because we have an important rendezvous point on the other side, and the alternative is to meet on the surface, where if the Regime doesn't find us, pirates will."

"But why do we need to meet anyone at all?"

"There are a few bits and bobs we need for the

war effort."

"You mean, for your new toys?"

Rommond stared coolly at Jacob. "When we field them, Jacob, the Regime won't see them like that at all."

The Lifemaker drifted slowly through the maze of mines. Though Rommond wanted to spare the energy reserves, they kept every light on full, shining in almost every direction, and always illuminating a dangerously close mine. Though there were six large air tanks on board, some of it was spared by their unnerving journey. The voyage would take one hundred leagues, and that was a long time to hold one's breath.

Taberah was appointed as the new sonar officer, because, in Rommond's words, she was "a good listener." She marked their journey on her map, periodically pointing out larger mines she had circled on the page earlier during their scouting mission. The submarine grazed one or two of these, and almost everyone, even Alson, closed their eyes at that moment before the expected explosion. But it did not come yet; the threat jumped from mine to mine, mocking them. The further they advanced without issue, the more they grew to fear that the stakes were higher. In a sea of a thousand mines, the crew of the Lifemaker had to be lucky a thousand times, but in that same sea, the Regime only had to be lucky once.

They travelled fifty leagues without issue, but now they were faced with a hurdle. Perhaps it was a mistake in Taberah's documenting, or perhaps it was the shifting waters, but a line of mines blocked the next part of their journey, and there did not appear to be any way around. The Lifemaker ground to a halt once more.

"So we go back?" Jacob wondered.

"No," Taberah said, as if this was a matter of pride. "Let's push on."

Rommond looked grave. "Tabs, mines aren't exactly things we want to push at all."

"I said we'd probably have to nudge one or two out of the way, so let's do that," Taberah proposed. "You've got a few small submersibles, right?"

Rommond shook his head. "I won't allow it."

"You'll have to tie me to the mast to stop me," she said.

Rommond looked as though he were contemplating it, but Jacob thought that even if he did, she would just chew through the ropes.

They gathered in the submersible pod bay, where they were greeted with tiny one-man crafts, globular in shape, powered by pedals and propellers, and looking decidedly ancient in comparison to the Lifemaker.

"These are powered by your own arms and legs," Rommond said. "There is no steam, no electricity, no diesel. You'll have a single oil lamp inside for light, and otherwise you'll need to rely on the beams from the Lifemaker. There's only enough oxygen for fifteen minutes. I have to emphasise this, Tabs, because I'm not sure you fully acknowledge the risk: if you get a cramp, if you can no longer pedal, if you run out of your own steam, you won't be able to make it back to us, and you'll die out there."

"I know the risks," Taberah said.

Whistler looked up at Rommond, who looked back down at him with equally worried eyes. "Perhaps if we wait a few days we can rig something up so the submersibles can power themselves," the general said.

"We can't afford to wait," Taberah replied. "What if the mines drift towards us? They're all around us now. We push on, and push through, or we perish."

"You're pregnant, Tabs," Rommond said, as if she needed reminding. "You're not just risking your life. You're risking the baby's. We can't afford to take those risks. Humanity can't."

"You have a saying, Rommond," she rejoined. "*You know my mind on this.*"

And it seemed in Rommond's resigned expression that he did indeed know her mind, and that they had had these kinds of disagreements in the past, and she had done what she wanted anyway, even in direct defiance of Rommond's orders. The general looked to Jacob, as if he thought that he might have better luck with her.

"I'll go with you," Jacob volunteered. It probably was not what the general had in mind.

"There's only room enough in each submersible for one," she replied.

"But there's more than one of them."

"The more of you out there," Rommond said, "the more chance we'll trigger an explosion." Jacob wondered if the general would rather he go instead of Taberah. In fact, he was certain of it.

"Yes, and the less of us out there," Jacob replied,

"the more chance we won't get those mines out of the way at all."

"So be it," the general acknowledged. "But let me warn you again, in case your ghost ever tries to condemn me: you will have fifteen minutes out there total—not fifteen to do the job, but fifteen to do the job and get back. After that, you will only have as long as you can hold your breath."

Chapter Eight

FIFTEEN MINUTES

Jacob immediately regretted volunteering as soon as he jammed himself inside one of the submersibles. It so was tiny it made his quarters look and feel like a palace. Within minutes his legs already felt a hint of a cramp, which was not reassuring, given how much he would come to rely on them to pedal that ball of metal and glass.

Perhaps Taberah was also complaining in her submersible, but it did not seem like it. Jacob presumed she had used these contraptions before.

"You know how to steer it?" Rommond asked Jacob.

"It looks simple enough. Basically a bicycle in a ball."

"With a propeller," Rommond added. "Many thousand leagues beneath the sea."

"Yeah, I forgot about the sea part."

"Don't," Rommond cautioned.

"Don't worry. Something tells me it'll stick in my mind."

He was shown how to use the two mechanical arms on the front of the vessel, which were powered by levers on either side of those that steered the craft.

It was such a tight fit that the levers were very close to one another, making it very easy to pull the wrong one. *So much for the Resistance's fabled engineering*, he thought. He patted his legs. *It's all about muscle and stamina now.*

"Should this lamp be burning now?" Jacob asked. The oil-lamp had already been lit for several minutes, and it dangled above the dashboard, faintly illuminating the meagre controls. There was no room for a spare lamp, or spare fuel. There was barely enough space for the one, and for Jacob's head, which banged against the lamp from time to time. Jacob could not help but think of the submersible as being like a coffin. He hoped it would not end up being true.

"Don't worry," Rommond said. "You'll run out of air before that light goes out."

With those final words, the door was closed and sealed air-tight. Though this was reassuring, to save Jacob being killed by the immense pressure, or by drowning, it also started the clock ticking away on the air supply, counting down to his untimely death. He glanced once at the chronometer on the ever so close dashboard, before feeling a sudden jerk as the submersible was pushed into a tube, which was then sealed off on the inside. Another door on the outside of the tube opened, flooding it with water, which buoyed the submersible and brought it into the black sea.

Then Jacob began pedalling, and the propeller set in motion. The submersible glided out of the tube and into the great emptiness of the ocean, which was not empty at all, but filled with many bobbing bombs, which Jacob and Taberah pedalled towards, instead of away from. Jacob decided to pedal at an even pace, to save his strength, but part of him felt like giving it his all, knowing that his all might end in several minutes' time.

The gloom around him made him appreciate more the glimmer of his oil lamp.

"Hell, this is dark," he said. He liked the darkness, but this was oppressing. It almost flooded his being. He was afraid that even when he returned to the light—or *if* he returned to the light—he would still feel that darkness in his soul.

He caught sight of Taberah's submersible leaving another tube, illuminated by one of the Lifemaker's blinding lights.

"The Lightmaker," Jacob quipped. He was not sure who he was talking to.

Taberah led the way to the mines in front of the submarine. They were further away than Jacob thought, and the Lifemaker's immense size was better appreciated when he had to pedal half its length to get to the front of it. He was already panting. It was a frightening feeling, because not only was he tired, but he thought the pants might be consuming more of that precious, and dwindling, supply of oxygen.

They reached the mines, which were slightly larger than the submersibles were, yet they looked monstrously large compared to how they looked from the Lifemaker. Taberah was already using the mechanical arms to stretch forth and gentle nudge one of the mines to the side.

Jacob glanced at the chronometer. Almost six

minutes had passed, and only one of the mines was out of the way. To the Resistance, Jacob was a newfound ally; Time was not.

He fiddled with the levers that controlled the mechanical arms of his craft. They sprang into action, and their sudden, jerky movements made Jacob afraid that they might suddenly clatter off a mine, and so be the end of them, and him.

He heard the metal fingers scratching off the metal of the mine. Each scrape almost sounded like the countdown of a bomb. Five. The mine was not budging. Four. He had to pedal a little more, to push it forward. Three. He had to be careful he did not pedal too much. Two. He had to let it drift away a little of its own accord. One. He had to hope it did not collide with another mine behind it.

Zero. There was no explosion. He was still alive. But a different counter was ticking away. Only eight minutes of oxygen remained.

Taberah had already cleared two of the mines by the time Jacob was starting on his second. He saw her whizzing over to a third. It was just those last two to go. And then get back. Perhaps the mines were not the trouble. It was getting back in time.

But this second mine seemed heavier than the first, or maybe Jacob was just more tired. He pushed the mechanical hands against it, but it would not budge. He was afraid to apply too much force, in case it would trigger an explosion. He withdrew slightly and pushed against it once more, but it drifted only a little, and at this position it could still tear a hole in the Lifemaker. He retreated again, and pedalled more fiercely, but still the mine was stubborn.

The sweat rolled down Jacob's forehead. It made an ocean on his palms. The chronometer showed just five and a half minutes remaining. Time was the greatest pressure beneath the sea.

Then Taberah's submersible appeared beside him, and she nudged the mine with him, and it moved a little more. They withdrew and tried again, and they cleared it out of the way of the Lifemaker.

The job was done. But their struggle was not over yet.

They turned their crafts around, and the turning felt like the slow revolution of a globe. It seemed like it took every minute they had remaining. Jacob glanced at the counter once more. Three minutes and twenty seconds.

He began to pedal frantically, and he saw that Taberah was lagging behind. He slowed down for her, as if that would help, and she waved her hand to him, as if to tell him to keep going, with or without her. He felt torn, but the chronometer bade him swear allegiance, and his feet struck the pedals as if his life depended on it. It did.

Two minutes. He could no longer see Taberah. He thought for a moment he could go back and push her, but he knew he did not have enough time, or enough energy. His legs began to ache. His hands clung to the steering sticks, as if the tighter his clutch, the faster his speed.

Then the light dimmed above him, and he glanced up to see the withering flame. *Hell*, he thought, as if the flame was disappearing to join its relatives in that damned place. He remembered, and cursed, Rommond's words: *You'll run out of air before that light goes out.* Part of him wanted to get back just to tell the general he was wrong, but another part reminded him that he was already short of breath.

He put every ounce of his energy, every pound of strength, into working the pedals. The aches in his legs grew, and the light dimmed. He did not think he could go any faster, but he pedalled as if Death were advancing behind him.

Yet the faster he went, the more the light flickered, until, at that last glance, it seemed that Death had arrived to snuff it out.

"No, no, no," Jacob pleaded.

But the light went out.

"Damn!" he said in the darkness—*to* the darkness.

He no longer knew exactly where to go, for the submarine's lights did not illuminate the hatch leading back inside. It was all a guess, and it was a guessing game that afforded very little time, but the very big prize of life, or the consolation of death.

He could not tell, but it must have been less than a minute to go. He had paid more attention to the dwindling flame, not the dwindling seconds.

Suddenly he caught a glimmer of a light to his side. He was not certain, but he presumed it was Taberah. He hoped it was not that fabled light that those near to death spoke of. Either way, he turned the vessel towards it and began to pedal like crazy.

It must have been less than thirty seconds by now. He kept pedalling, but he found it harder than ever. He felt he could not get enough air into his lungs. They began to burn as much as the muscles in his legs. The vessel grew very hot. The darkness grew thicker, and the lights of the Lifemaker seemed to dim.

Jacob felt himself fading out of consciousness. By now it must have been seconds to go. Maybe they had already passed.

There was a moment, which seemed to last forever, where he felt a great regret. He thought of wasted opportunities, of friendships he could no longer get back, and people he could no longer make amends with. Taberah came into his mind, and he wondered if she had escaped the sea, and if her child—*his* child— would grow up without him. His regret was greater than his fear, and his fear was greater than his pain.

Then everything turned to a deeper shade of black.

He held his breath, and the darkness consumed him.

Chapter Nine

PROMISE

Jacob awoke in his quarters, with far too many people crammed inside, standing over and staring at him. Doctor Mudro was there, paying more attention to his pipe than his patient. Rommond was there, looking as immovable as ever. Whistler was there, with worry seeping through his bandages. And Taberah was there, alive and well—more alive and more well than Jacob felt.

"So I guess we made it," he said, though really he would have liked the confirmation.

"No," Rommond said. "We hauled you in."

"I *pushed* you in," Taberah said. "We tried to revive you in the submersible bay."

"Maybe I just needed a bit of Mudro's leaf." He smiled at Taberah. "Or the kiss of life."

"And why would you presume that I, and not the doctor, granted it?" Taberah replied.

Mudro grinned, and playfully raised his eyebrows.

"Well, whoever it was," Jacob said, "thanks."

"Come on, then, let's give him some breathing space," Rommond said. Jacob thought that maybe he just did not like spending too long in the same room as him. Mudro left with him, leaving Taberah and

Whistler behind.

"That was close," Jacob said.

"A bit too close for comfort," Taberah replied.

"When have we ever been concerned with comfort?"

"Says the man we carried to his bed."

"At least it wasn't my grave."

This latter comment forced Whistler to turn away. He looked out the window, as if he was still trying to find those unusual fishes. There was only darkness out there now. Even the night sky was brighter. Yet it was a long time ago since they had seen the sky.

Taberah placed her hand on Jacob's shoulder. "You did good out there," she said, and her voice was softer. Jacob was not the only one who noticed, because Whistler looked at her too.

"So did you," Jacob replied.

"I need to get back to the command centre to guide us through the remaining mines. But maybe," and she paused, "maybe we can meet for dinner. Just the two of us. Not today, of course, but maybe in a few days?"

"I'd like that," Jacob said.

Taberah smiled and left the room.

Whistler loitered a little longer, standing awkwardly by the door, as if he expected to be told to leave at any moment. "I guess I'm not the only one who's unlucky," he said.

"I'm still alive," Jacob retorted with a smile. "We both are."

"I guess."

Jacob laughed. "Don't tell me you missed me for

those fifteen minutes."

Whistler did not respond.

"I was always coming back, you know," Jacob said. He knew that was not true.

"For your money?" Whistler asked, and he bit his lip tightly, as if to punish his mouth.

Cheeky, Jacob thought. He had actually forgotten about the chest of coils, tucked away safely beneath his metal bed. He had not thought of it when death was near. Perhaps that was because Heaven was too expensive, and Hell was free.

"I couldn't leave you to do all the mischief on your own, now could I?" Jacob said.

Whistler forced a smile.

"Besides," Jacob continued, "I'm sure there are more fishes down here to spot. First one to spot them all wins a prize."

Whistler glanced at the window. "In the dark?"

"We can't make it too easy now, can we?"

Whistler rolled his eyes, but smiled anyway. "Well, um, I guess I'll let you get some rest."

"I've probably had enough shut-eye for now."

"Jacob," Whistler said, stalling at the door.

"Yes?"

"Will you promise me you'll always come back?"

Jacob paused longer than he thought he should. This did not feel like just another idle question; it was a solemn oath. "I promise," he said eventually. But he did not know if he could keep it.

Chapter Ten

TREASURE HUNT

Under Taberah's guidance, and Alson's careful steering, the Lifemaker cleared the mine field two days later. By this time Jacob was feeling much better, far too well to not be causing trouble somewhere on the ship. He remembered Taberah's dinner offer, so he thought he would surprise her by organising something a little special.

He recruited Whistler, who was more than willing, to help him find some items for the romantic meal, which Jacob thought that even Rommond might have described as "perfect." Jacob could see it in his mind: an ornate tablecloth, half a dozen candles, half a crate of roses, the finest cutlery, the choicest china, the tastiest meal, the tastier dessert, and Taberah and himself decked out in their finery, sipping wine and toasting to the success of a month beneath the sea, and a month closer to the birth of a new child, for them and for the other Pure on board.

But there was a problem.

The submarine did not exactly have all of those items available, and for those that were, they were not exactly easy to acquire. There was no flower shop, no butcher's, and no baker's. The few flowers that were on board were made of wax, and, while Jacob thought that they could double up as candles, killing two birds with one stone was not exactly a romantic gesture. Those flowers were also closely hoarded, and the candles were adored and worshipped like idols, for, after all, they invoked the gods of light. The chef's assistant, who had more beard than belly, but had plenty of the latter too, demonstrated his skills by throwing cleavers in the direction of any who dared ask for more than they were rationed, and he also cast condemnations and allegations at anyone he thought might be the illusive pantry thief. As for the best china, that was in Rommond's possession, and Jacob had a feeling that the general might wage a war to keep it there.

The list Jacob had compiled was long, and so far he had ticked off nothing bar his shipmates. It was a disappointing and disheartening start, and Jacob hoped it was not an omen for his relationship with Taberah. He found himself questioning exactly what he was doing. He was never into romance. He never made big displays of affection. He felt the Resistance was having a greater effect on him than he previously thought.

Whistler made the finest gesture by gifting Jacob a small collection of spoons, the very same ones with which he had tried, rather unsuccessfully, to teach Jacob all about etiquette. Jacob offered him ten coils for these, but Whistler refused, insisting that he wanted them to be a gift. Jacob wondered if the boy also thought the coils were, in some way, cursed, and that he did not want to be as afflicted by them as

Jacob was. *There are worse afflictions*, Jacob mused.

Spoons alone would not make much of a dinner, however, so the duo set about trying to buy what they could from the willing, and sneak and swindle away what they could not. Jacob gave Whistler twenty coils as bargaining chips, and told him only to spend ten, which the boy immediately copped on to, refusing, once again, to be paid for his gift.

Jacob's first port of call was Soasa's door, which he banged on like a dynamite explosion. She opened it slowly with a sigh, and rolled her eyes when she saw Jacob standing there. She looked like she had been napping, but the black rings around her eyes were not just from sleep.

"Hope I didn't wake you," Jacob said. "Hell, what happened to you?"

"I got in a fight."

"Did you win?"

Soasa pouted. "Does it look like I won?"

"Well, I don't know, you could have given the other one more than two black eyes."

"No."

"Who was it with?"

"The Copper Matron."

"Ah," Jacob said. "I think I'd be lucky to come out with any eyes at all in a fight with her."

"I think so too."

"Cheeky," Jacob said. "So, what prompted this brawl?"

"We bumped into each other."

"That's it?"

"Jacob, I went with Taberah when the Resistance

split. The Matron doesn't forgive people like us as easily as Rommond does."

"Ah."

"Anyway, what do you want?"

"Not a fight, at least," Jacob said. She looked like she was more than ready for one. "I need a favour."

"Go to a different door then," Soasa replied, slamming hers on Jacob's foot.

"Yeah, you see, I have an offer."

"Make it elsewhere."

"It's worth a coil or too."

Soasa shrugged. "And where'll I spend it?"

"I don't know. The corner shop?

Soasa cocked her head.

"Maybe you can buy some mines from the Regime," Jacob said. "You like explosives, right?"

"Get to the point, Jacob."

"I need candles."

"Have you not tried the corner shop?" Soasa retorted.

"They're out. See, I thought that you might have access to the storage, what with you being Dynamite Lady and all."

"I can get candles," Soasa said. "But I only have access to the Order's supply. Rommond won't let me go near the Resistance stash. I guess there's still bad blood for us jumping ship."

"I just need two or three," Jacob said. "Maybe four. Hell, five will be plenty."

"I can get you three," Soasa said. "But it will cost you more than you're willing to pay, I bet."

"See, betting is my kind of game," Jacob said.

"How much do you bet I won't pay?"

Soasa smirked. "I bet you ten coils you won't pay my asking price."

"Challenge accepted. Now, how much for the candles?"

"An even hundred."

"Sheesh," Jacob said. "You know they're just wax, not iron, right?"

"Yes, and I know you want them bad," she replied. "And I also know you can afford it."

"All right then," Jacob said. "One hundred coils, minus the ten you lost on the bet."

"Happy to lose," she said. "I'll have the candles for you tonight."

Jacob thanked her and blew her a kiss, before running off.

"Jacob," Soasa called after him. "If this is for Taberah ... don't bother."

"What do you mean?" he asked as he came back.

"She's using you."

Jacob stopped; his heart followed. "How?"

"She doesn't love you, Jacob."

"Maybe I don't love her."

"Candles?" Soasa said, raising an eyebrow. "Don't tell me you're smuggling love poems as well."

"More like dirty limericks."

"Do you know how many men she's been through trying to get pregnant for the cause? She hasn't exactly been 'pure' since Whistler's birth. You're just warm blood, Jacob. To her you're just a means to an end, a necessity of the time being. A soldier who can easily be disposed of."

"And what are you?" Jacob asked.

"A soldier with bombs."

"Well, I still have plenty of uses."

"And when you don't?"

"We'll see when the time comes."

Soasa looked him up and down, and there was pity in her eyes. "That time, Jacob, might come sooner than you think."

Whistler was very productive with his time, and many people were most obliging with his requests, especially when he did not mention the items were for Jacob. The boy procured a few fake flowers, much to his embarrassment as he was frequently asked if he had a girlfriend on board, and he also acquired one of the finer tablecloths from the officers' dining room.

Jacob was not having much luck on the higher decks, so he tried his chances on the floor of the Copper Vixens. As he skulked about, disguising his footsteps in the sound of hammers and drills from the female mechanics, he stumbled across a hatch leading down into the ironworks, where Rommond's prized vehicles were kept. As he placed his hand upon the handle of the hatch, he was stopped by the general, who pointed to a nearby sign.

"That floor is off limits," Rommond said. "It's lucky I was passing by."

Jacob grinned. *Sure*, he thought. *Just passing by.*

"The signage is there for a reason," the general stated.

Jacob looked at the large yellow letters on the

sign: *Forbidden.*

"You know, that's kind of like: *Welcome*," he said.

"In the language of the underworld, perhaps," Rommond replied. "But he who knows not when to obey shall find that he is really obeying his rebellious lower aspects. So then, is he really a rebel at all?"

Jacob took some pride in that description, and showed it with a grin. "Are we not part of a rebellion then? Or would you rather we obey you instead of the Iron Emperor?"

Rommond stared at him, but did not reply.

Jacob rapped his knuckles on the hatch; the sound echoed through the submarine.

"So, what are you cooking up down there? Are you building me a bigger room?"

"A smaller cell," Rommond said, "or your own private submarine."

"As long as I don't have to pedal."

The nervous chef, who made everyone else nervous, especially while wielding meat cleavers, was surprisingly obliging to Jacob's requests. He told him how he planned a romantic meal, and the chef got very excited about the prospects, digging out old recipe books and sharing how he was delighted to have the opportunity to craft something a little more exotic than the usual fare.

The final challenge was a raid of Rommond's china supply, tucked away in a locked cupboard in the farthest corner of his quarters. Jacob called this the *Curious Case of the Robbery of Rommond*, while

Whistler dubbed it the *Likely Case Where We Get Caught*.

"I don't think we should be doing this," Whistler protested. "Rommond will be furious."

"Only if he finds out."

"That's the bit I'm worried about."

"It's not like he's going to send us to the firing squad."

"I don't know," Whistler said. "He might send you."

Despite Whistler's concerns, it did not take much for Jacob to convince him. *Every kid needs a bit of adventure*, Jacob thought. *Hell, every adult needs some too.*

The plot was simple: Whistler would sneak inside and grab the prized china, and Jacob would stand watch, distracting any passers-by with his guile and charm.

"Why I am the smuggler?" Whistler asked. "I'd be a better lookout."

"I've got better eyesight."

"No you don't."

"I can whistle the warning signal better."

Whistler smirked and shook his head.

They timed the burglary for when Rommond was on duty, but the problem with that plan, which Whistler pointed out at the onset, was that the general was always on duty, and he considered the entire submarine as the location of his shift. While he was often in the control room, he wandered the decks almost as often as Jacob did—possibly in pursuit.

On this occasion, however, Rommond was not in

his quarters, and the door was unlocked. Jacob had observed previously that the general never locked his room, and no one dared enter it without his permission.

"I feel guilty already," Whistler whispered as he took a single foot inside the room. The door creaked, like a burglar alarm. The boy froze, and Jacob could see that he was staring at the Brooklyn plaque across the room. There was something sacred about the place, like a monastery—or a mausoleum.

"This isn't right," Whistler said, coming back to the door. "I can't do it."

"We're just borrowing a few cups and bowls," Jacob said. "Rommond did say: *Make yourself at home*."

"Not in his room!"

"Okay, okay! You be the lookout and I'll sneak inside."

Whistler agreed to this, but was as nervous outside the room as inside. He continuously urged Jacob to hurry up, and awkwardly tried to look like he was doing something other than loitering outside the general's abode.

Then Rommond appeared at the end of the corridor, pausing to chat briefly with Lieutenant Tradam. Whistler panicked and waved at Jacob, who was poised precariously on a chair and reaching up to one of the top shelves of the cupboard, where the china was sealed in a box that was clipped into place to stop it from moving. Jacob was giving all his attention to unclipping it, and none to Whistler's frantic gestures.

The boy then tried to whistle, but, despite his name, was miserable at it. He made vague airy noises, more like a gentle breeze, which did nothing to steal Jacob's gaze. He then tried whispering, and then murmuring a little louder, until finally it seemed like he would have to shout, when Rommond began walking towards him.

Whistler did not know what to do. He contemplated running, and screaming while he ran, or charging into Rommond's room and barricading himself inside, where he could then await his punishment with his fellow prisoner. He thought of leaning against the wall and playing it cool, and feigning complete surprise and shock when Jacob was found inside, but he did not think he could pull that off. He even considered telling Rommond everything, or of blaming Jacob on it all, but he knew for certain he could not live with the guilt.

"Whistler, young chap," Rommond said as he approached. "What are you doing here?"

Whistler stumbled with his words. "I … uh … we … I … was just …" He had to stop himself mid-breath. He thought he might be having a heart attack. He thought that if he was, it might be a good distraction.

"I presume you were just passing through," Rommond suggested.

"Yes!" Whistler exclaimed. "Passing through. Just passing through."

The general gave a hint of a smile. "On your way to visit Jacob, perhaps?"

"Yep. That's where I was going."

Whistler saw Jacob nearing the door, loot in

hand. The boy, in alarm, pointed down the corridor to where Rommond had come from, and the general looked in that direction.

"I think Lieutenant Tradam is calling," Whistler said.

"He's not," Rommond stated, "but maybe you have better ears than I."

Jacob hurried out of the room and down the opposite corridor while the general was not looking, and Whistler felt a great relief, which he thought might feel greater if he could now escape the general's company.

"Well, I better go then."

"Very well," Rommond said. "Brogan," he added, as the boy skipped down the corridor in a frenzy. Whistler turned to him with nervous eyes. "Tell Jacob to have them back by tomorrow."

Night fell, though the eternal darkness of the sea did not show it. Jacob and Whistler stood back to admire their handiwork. They had conjured up a romantic meal that even Mudro could not have made appear from nowhere. The coil crate turned into a table, disguised by a red tablecloth, laced around the edges. The candles burned brightly, reflected by a small mirror so as to give the illusion that there were more of them. The light illuminated Karlsif's freshly-prepared meal, which steamed up the glass coverings. Wine was on hand, and roses were on display. The oil lamps were turned down low.

A note was sent to the control room, where Taberah was stationed. She was due to end her shift any minute now.

"We did it," Jacob said.

Whistler smiled broadly.

"Now it's time to see its effects," Jacob said.

"Have fun!" Whistler cheered, before heading off, as proud as ever.

Jacob sat down and waited for Taberah. His quarters were tiny, and not ideal for a dinner, but with all of these embellishments, the room looked *cosy* instead. Some people would have paid good money to be that close to someone. Jacob found it somewhat amusing that his own money had not bought him most of these items, and that the crate of coils was better served as a table.

He took out his pocket watch. *7:01pm. She should be just finishing up*. It would take a few minutes for her to make it down to his quarters. *7:10pm. Any minute now.*

He began to rehearse in his mind what he would say to her, how he would tell her that he felt he was somehow changing, and that she was the instrument of that change. He went through so many versions of his speech, thinking some too soppy, and others too cold, until he realised that he still did not really know what it was about her that made him go through so much trouble for a little candlelit dinner in his room.

He sent another note, and then waited fifteen minutes, until the food was cold; and then thirty minutes, until the wine was warm; and then for an hour, until the candles burned low. He waited long enough for him to forget his rehearsed speeches, and he continued to wait some more, even though by now he knew she was not coming.

He caught the fading glimmer of the candle flame in the mirror, and he caught the broken expression on his face. He always was alone—he *liked* to be alone—but this time the solitude stung him deep. The emptiness filled his heart, just like the growing darkness filled the room.

Chapter Eleven

DELUGE

Wine was not Jacob's poison, but he drank it all, and then decided to while away the evening with a stroll through the submarine. He was not exactly looking for trouble, but he had a feeling that trouble liked to take a stroll of its own. He was glad he was not on a rocking boat, because he brought a glass of whiskey with him. There was something about being beneath the ocean that was thirsty work, even if he was not exactly helpful to the crew.

During his wanderings, he found Whistler peeping through a slightly ajar door on the top deck. It was not until Jacob sneaked up behind him that he could see that the boy was eavesdropping on Taberah and Rommond.

"I was wondering where you were," Jacob said.

Whistler jumped and turned to Jacob with a panicked expression. He glanced up and down, and left and right, as if to suggest that he was looking everywhere bar the room he had been spying on.

"Didn't your mother tell you that it's rude to spy on people?" Jacob asked, which did not help Whistler's nervous reaction. "Without the appropriate apparatus, that is," Jacob added, gulping down the last of his whiskey and pressing the glass to the wall, and his ear to the glass.

Whistler simpered, but he still looked like he had been caught red-handed.

"Sounds like … mumble mumble," Jacob said.

"I wasn't spying," Whistler blurted.

"Relax, kid. I wouldn't care if you were."

"But I wasn't."

"Well, I'm not spying either," Jacob said, before taking a glance through the door. Maybe it was the whiskey, but he could have sworn that he saw Taberah consoling Rommond. "Strange," he said, almost involuntarily.

"It's not strange," Whistler said, and he sounded hurt.

"Are you seeing what I'm seeing?"

"She's always nice to him," Whistler whispered.

"That's not what I heard," Jacob said.

"What do you mean?"

"Well, the attempted coup."

"It wasn't a coup."

"Right. Not if it didn't work."

Whistler's eyes started to water.

"Are you okay?" Jacob asked.

Whistler looked like he was going to say something, but his lip trembled instead. He turned and ran off, leaving a trail of tears behind him.

What did I say? Jacob thought. He glanced back into the room, where Taberah had her arm around Rommond's shoulders. *Or what did he see?*

It did not take much detective work to surmise that Whistler had retreated to his quarters. Jacob would have normally left people to their own devices, especially if they wanted to water those devices with their tears, but he could not help but feel sorry for the lad, and feel that maybe he really needed a friend. On board the Lifemaker, that did not exactly leave many options. So, Jacob sauntered down to the next deck where their quarters were.

"Can I come in?" he asked. He did not get an answer, but the door was also slightly ajar, as if Whistler was hoping he would do some eavesdropping of his own. Jacob entered the room to find Whistler face down on his bed, smothering his sorrows. Jacob preferred whiskey for that.

"Do you want to talk about it?" Jacob offered, feeling more than a little awkward as he did. It was not his usual line. He preferred: *Do you want to pay for that?*

Whistler did not respond, or if he did, his words were muffled by the bed sheets.

Jacob stood by the door, pursing his lips. It was easier than actually saying anything. Hell, smuggling amulets was easier than finding out what was bothering the boy. Jacob found himself staring out the window into the blackness of the sea, silently hoping he would see some unusual fish that he could distract Whistler with.

But nothing happened, and Whistler was not forthcoming on his own. He did glance up from time to time, as if to check that Jacob was still there, but all Jacob could hear was the odd sob or sigh, the vocabulary of sorrow.

When the silence became too much, Jacob broke

it by dragging his heels across the room. He would have dragged a chair out to sit on, but the rooms were barely big enough for a bed. He slumped down on the end of the bed, making sure to stretch his arms and make it clear that he was going to sit on anyone below if they did not move out of the way. Whistler rolled away just in time, revealing his tear-covered face.

"You're not supposed to get your bandages wet," Jacob said.

Whistler pouted.

"Come on, kid, tell me what's up."

There was no longer enough space for Whistler to roll around and bury his face again, but he was still struggling with his lips to form the words of whatever was bothering him.

Jacob decided to try to make it easier for the boy. "Okay, let's make a deal—a smuggler's trade, as it were. I'll tell you something that bothers me, and then it's your turn. Deal?" He held out his hand, and Whistler reluctantly shook it. It was much easier than speaking.

"So," Jacob began, "I never really fell in love before, and then I met your mother, and I don't know what it is about her, but something just clicks. It's like … it's kind of like cogs fitting together. But the thing about cogs is that you can easily jam something in between them, and everything grinds to a halt. So here I see her with Rommond, and I think … is he the iron bar that's jammed between our cogs?"

He did not intend to say any of that. He expected to make something up, to tell some paltry invented trouble that he half-expected Whistler to see through, and fully hoped that it would not matter. It might have been hard for Whistler to talk, but it seemed that it was easier for Jacob than he anticipated. He blamed the whiskey.

"It's not like that," Whistler said meekly. He seemed a little amused by Jacob's tale.

"What do you mean?"

"I mean … he's not interested in her."

"Well, she seems plenty interested in him. Is that what's bothering you?"

"Kind of."

"Do you not like him?"

"I do. I think he's cool. But—"

"But what?"

"She's never … never there like that for me."

Jacob did not know what to say to that.

"Sometimes I feel like," Whistler stuttered, "sometimes I feel like she doesn't care, that … that I'm just like a tool, something useful for the Order. And sometimes I think that maybe she'll get rid of me when I stop being useful, and I keep failing and causing trouble. It's my fault we're even down here! And … and I keep thinking that maybe the next mistake I make will be the last one, and she won't want me any more, and I don't want to feel like that." By this point he was almost bawling, and the bandages on his face were soaked through. Jacob placed his hand upon the boy's shoulder, and he felt the child tremble, as if he had never been comforted before.

Hell, was all Jacob could think of, but he was glad he did not say it. "I think she does care, Whistler. Maybe she's not the best at showing it, but I think she really does care. And I don't think you need to worry about being thrown aside. Hell, I'm still here, and I'm useless."

"But sometimes she won't even look at me," Whistler continued, as if the dam could no longer hold back the deluge. "It's like she can't stand the sight of me. It's like … it's like I make her feel bad, and I don't want to make people feel bad."

If there was some place lower than Hell, Jacob would have said its name in his mind right now. Again he was glad his tongue was more comforting than his thoughts. "You don't make people feel bad, kid. Honestly, you don't. Look, Whistler, when we were in the Hold, you were the only thing that kept me from going mad. In the darkness of that cell, you were the only light. I've achieved all sorts in my life, but I've got nothing on you. Hell, it was worth getting caught just to have bumped into you."

He smiled, and Whistler smiled. But the flood-gates were open, and Whistler had more to say.

"I don't blame her," the boy said. "I think … I sometimes can't even look at myself in the mirror."

"You shouldn't worry about the scars—"

"But this … this was before then."

"Well, you're not ugly, if that's what you mean."

"It's not that."

"What is it then?"

"It's just … it's like … the odd time I think I see something else."

"What do you mean?" Jacob asked. He felt suddenly on edge.

"You know how I … how I got my name?"

"The blowing the whistle thing?"

"When I see one of them, the demons," Whistler stammered, "I get this funny feeling. And sometimes, not all the time, but sometimes, when I look at … at myself … I get that same feeling too."

Chapter Twelve

DESTITUTE

Jacob did not know how to truly comfort Whistler. He was not really the listening type, and he found that he had to give some kind of response, just to break those tense moments of silence. He assured the boy that he must have been imaging things, and suggested that if Whistler's natural ability to identify the demons could be wrong, as it had proven to be several times before, then it was likely wrong again. This appeared to help, and the flood of tears that came from Whistler ceased to flow. Jacob stayed with him for a while, until he fell asleep, and then headed back to his own quarters, where he unearthed one of the bottles of wine from his planned dinner. After listening to Whistler's sorrows, he really thought he needed another drink. It was not long before he was several glasses in, and feeling like he still could not quench his thirst.

By the sixth glass, his room began to feel too small, as if he was trapped in a glass of his own. He staggered outside and found his way to Taberah's quarters, where he set up patrol outside. He stumbled back and forth, glass and bottle in hand, warding off any passers-by, some of whom walked by all the quicker. Jacob mumbled something as they passed, which might have been an insult, or a threat, or his best attempt at poetry. When he could no longer patrol, he camped outside the room, clinging to the wine bottle as if it could pour out coils.

After several hours, Taberah finally returned to her quarters, finding Jacob asleep against the door. She pushed it open, and Jacob collapsed onto the ground, waking with a snort. He yawned and stretched, and raised his glass to Taberah from his vantage point on the ground.

"G'morning," he slurred.

"It's midnight," Taberah said.

"G'night!" Jacob cheered. "To each and every one!"

"Dear lord," Taberah said, stepping over him to get into her room.

"Oo aar! Good job you're wearing trousers," Jacob said with a laugh. He rolled over and dragged himself into the room with his arms. "More women should wear trousers. I've always said it. Didn't I always say it?"

"What are you doing here, Jacob?" Taberah asked, slamming her diary down on the table.

"Waiting for you, m'darling!" Jacob said, with a hiccup. "I got you … I got you this." He held up the empty bottle. "Dunno what happened, hic, to it. Thieves!" He sat up and pointed at random spots in the room. "They're everywhere."

"I think we better get you sobered up."

Taberah helped Jacob up, which was a struggle, and plopped him in a chair, where it was a struggle to keep him. He kept getting up and wandering about, and reaching for the wine bottle, and raising a fist to the heavens when discovering, time and time again, that it was empty.

She made a pot of tea, and assured Jacob that each cup had whiskey in it, and he swamped down half a dozen cups of it, while Taberah sipped at one. In time he fell asleep, waking several hours later to find that Taberah was still up. She was writing in her diary.

"*October 18th, 12:00am*," Jacob said. "*I met a drunk today.*"

"Funny that," Taberah replied. "I met one too."

"Sorry," he said. "I guess I got a little carried away."

"You're not the first to hit the bottle too hard, Jacob."

"At least it didn't break," he said, holding up the culprit.

"It might have been better if it had broken while there was still half the liquor inside."

"I probably would have found another one. Turns out Karlsif has quite a store. A crate of coils comes in handy then."

"I'm sure it does," Taberah said, closing her diary.

"So why aren't you in bed?"

"A drunk is keeping me awake."

"Again, sorry about that."

"What did you come here for, Jacob?"

"Did you not get my note?"

"What note?"

"The invitation to dinner."

"Yes, I got that."

"And the second one?"

"I got that too," Taberah acknowledged.

"And?"

"I was busy."

"You could have said."

"Jacob," she said sternly, "unlike you, I have duties on this ship."

"Is consoling Rommond one of them?"

"What is *that* supposed to mean?"

"I don't know. You spend more time with him than anyone else."

"We're old friends, Jacob, and we're both leaders in this war. And anyway, I don't need to justify who I spend my time with, least of all to you."

"What about Whistler?"

"What about him?"

"Exactly!" Jacob exclaimed. "That's your attitude with him in general. And if you're not ignoring him, it's like you hate the kid."

Taberah shifted uneasily in her seat. "I don't hate him."

"Well, you sure as hell aren't making it clear that you love him either."

Taberah paused. "It's complicated, Jacob."

"How is it? He's your kid. You gotta love your kid."

"Will you love yours?" she asked.

"You know, I mightn't make much of a father, but hell, I'll love the tyke, sure."

"You say that now." She looked away, as if the thought of love stung deep.

"Did you not say it when you were pregnant with

Whistler?"

"I said it, yes."

"And did you not mean it?"

Taberah look away again, before returning her fiery gaze. "He isn't your child, Jacob."

"The way you go on, he might as well not be yours either!"

"You've gotten high and mighty all of a sudden, Jacob. What gives you the right to be throwing stones?"

"I don't pretend to be perfect," Jacob said, "but I do try."

"And what do you think any of us are doing?"

"Well, it seems like you're ignoring the people who care about you."

"How?"

"I went out of my way today," Jacob said, "to make something special."

"I didn't ask for anything special."

"You said you wanted dinner."

"I was just being polite."

"And were you just being polite when you slept with me?"

She rolled her eyes. "Jacob, I barely knew you. I still don't."

"Then *get* to know me."

"I am," she said, "and I'm not liking this side of you."

"What, the side that cares? The side that loves?"

Taberah paused, biting her lip. "I like you, Jacob … but I don't love you."

"Well, that's clear."

"I don't think you really love me either."

Jacob sighed. "Maybe not."

"It's hard for me to fall in love, Jacob. I'm not sure I really love anyone. Rommond's probably the closest."

"What about Whistler? Hell, Taberah, that kid thinks you'll cast him aside as soon as he stops being useful."

"It's not like that."

"And what about me? Are you just using me?"

"Jacob, we're fighting a war. There's a bigger picture out there than you and me. I don't have time to be worrying about your problems."

"But you have time for Rommond," Jacob said. "How's that?"

"Jacob, he lost *everything*. He's only ever loved one person, and he lost him. I'm amazed he's holding it together so well. Do you know what would happen if he crumbled? The Resistance would fall apart. They rally to him. If he goes down, we all go down with him. I cannot let that happen."

"So it's all about business then."

"It's about life, Jacob. Our survival. *That's* the bigger picture that you're not seeing."

"The big picture is made up of lots of little pictures, Taberah. You can't just think of the wider war and ignore all the people fighting in it. We matter."

"It wasn't so long ago that you said you didn't care about the war."

"I care about the people."

"Funny that," Taberah said. "To everyone else it looks like you only care about the coils."

"You're all about the low blows, aren't you?"

"It wouldn't hurt if it wasn't true."

"Do you want to know why coils mean so much to me, huh?"

"I'd like to hear your excuse, sure."

"It's not an excuse, Taberah."

"I'm listening." She poured a fresh cup of tea, but Jacob did not touch it. She sipped at hers, staring at him over the rim of the cup as he recounted his past.

"I don't want the same fate as my father," Jacob said. "When I was a child, he was a giant of a man. He could command legions with his eyes, armies with his voice, could ask a god to bow down to him, and they would. Or so it seemed to me. He had everything, and I felt like I had everything because of him.

"But you know what they say about rose-tinted lenses. I didn't grow up. I didn't have time for that. I had the harsh realities of adulthood hoisted upon me overnight. By the time I found out that my father had no money at all, that he was living on loans, it was too late. He was locked up in a workhouse, and for a week I begged every god I could think of to let me see him again. And maybe they answered, because do you know what this messed up world did? They sent me to the workhouse too, along with my mother. Maybe that's what you'd call a family business, because we worked day and night to pay off his pennies. Nothing, it seemed, could pay off the pounds, not even when my mother collapsed and died of exhaustion. In time even my father could no longer lift the bricks or lay the tracks. Do you know that Iron Wall? We built the foundations for that, back before the demons came.

"It took me eight years to work off my father's debt, and by that time he wasn't just broke, he was broken. By then I wasn't even doing it for him, because I saw that everything he'd done for the first seven years of my life, everything I thought he had done for me and my mother, was a lie. I was fifteen when they let us out, and we had nowhere to go, and I was *damned* if I was going to work to pay my father's way again! Hell, I guess I was damned either way. I don't know where he went at the time, but I found him years later, when the Regime came into power. He was homeless, and he was hopeless, and when he first told me about the demons I thought it was the ramblings of a madman. Hell, sometimes I still do. To think that he was such a giant to me before, and then he was nothing—it crushed whatever was left of my heart.

"Those were the days when I learned the value of money. The only other kids I knew then were the other unlucky sods who were blamed for their parents' crimes. We never played. We worked. What got me most some days was when we toiled to make toys for other children to play with. Sometimes I tried to get an extra few seconds with one before the conveyor belt moved on, just an extra moment to hold that little wooden horse or toy soldier, so I could better imagine playing with it when I went to sleep. I didn't realise that we were also soldiers, fighting a war of wealth—only that those of us crushed beneath the boots of the rich worked to make them newer, heavier boots.

"So maybe now I can only see the thorns. But unlike the roses, I *felt* those thorns. I know that they're really out there. And that was all before the Harvest. So, you know, I don't hate the Regime like some other people do, like the Treasury probably does, because life for me before the Harvest wasn't any better. Hell, those people in the Treasury used to run the place back then. It was *them* who made the workhouse rules.

"And maybe something awakens in me when I see the dull glint of an iron coil, but that was something that has been sleeping ever since those days: hope. The demons might have their drug, and maybe this is mine, but I've already seen what happens when I don't take it. I've already had the bad trips. And maybe it's foolish of me to save up for a rainy day in a world of desert sand, but I've lived, and worked, through enough rainy days to feel the need to save up for an umbrella."

Taberah drank her tea slowly through this account, hiding her reaction behind her cup. Perhaps she did not want to show him any sympathy, and he did not want it, but he knew that something stirred in her, that as he almost relived those past hurts, she had to feel just a little of his pain. When he was finished, she was silent for a time, as if she was documenting his tale in the diary of her mind.

"The past is a dangerous thing," she said when the silence grew too deep. "How can you fight for the future when you're still fighting the past?"

"Maybe I don't want to fight for the future," he replied.

"Maybe you don't have a choice."

The silence returned for a moment, and then

suddenly the submarine began to sink, forcing Jacob and Taberah to clutch their seats. Their hearts sank with it, but fear beat a new rhythm into them, which quickened in pace as their vessel began to plummet at even greater speeds.

"What's going on?" Jacob asked. He hoped he was not still intoxicated. Yet it was perhaps a better thing if he was in the horrors of drink and not the horrors of where they plunging.

Taberah did not answer. She got up quickly and left the room, racing up to the command centre. Jacob called after her, but she was gone. He hurried back to his own quarters, which felt like they were falling away from him.

Everyone and everything was falling. Falling into the abyss.

Chapter Thirteen

ATTACK IN THE ABYSS

"We're sinking fast!" Alson cried. "I can't control it."

"How are we sinking?" Rommond asked. "Do we have a leak?" He nodded to one of his lieutenants, who hurried down to the lower levels to consult with Boulder, the submarine's chief mechanic, about possible damage to the hull.

"Someone's filled one of the ballast tanks," Alson said.

"What do you mean *someone*?"

"They don't just go off of their own accord, Rommond!"

"Well, blow the ballast," he ordered.

"I can't. None of the tanks appear to be connected with an air cannister any more."

Rommond turned to Tradam. "Get down there and see what's up." He grabbed the lieutenant by the shoulder before he could go. "And bring a gun."

The Lifemaker sank as if it were made of lead. There was no time, nor truly any viable way, to jettison anything, and even if every possession on board the submarine was discarded, the weight of the water in the ballast tanks alone would keep it buried at the bottom of the sea.

And it was to the bottom that the vessel now plunged, into the waters that were blacker than any black on land, into a gloom that was more consuming than the deepest night. Were the crew not focused on their frenzied work to stop the steep descent, they might have glanced out one of the many round windows, and they might have thought that they were looking into the black iris of an evil creature— and they might have been right.

As the vessel fell, the pressure rose. The hull began to creak as if held inside the crushing fist of a giant, or the chomping maw of a giant fish. The most senior officers were unperturbed by the groaning of the metal, for they knew that the hull was thick and could withstand the terrible pressures of the deep, but the confidence of many others was shaken when bolts burst out of their holdings, striking walls, breaking the glass of gaslights, and even hitting members of the crew with a most violent force.

The fall was so fast that Tradam found it difficult to get down to the ballast tank. He tried to walk, but instead he stumbled. He tried to run, but instead he fell. For every step forward, he was thrown back, or hurled against the hull, or cast against another crewman.

And then the submarine struck the ocean's floor, and if Tradam had not already been on the ground, he would have been knocked from his feet. He clambered up, and he raced to the back of the ship and burst through the huge metal door into a room full of cannisters and tanks.

It was very dark, so much so that he could barely make out the curved shapes around him. He reached up for an oil lamp, but his hand found nothing. Then he heard a faint footstep, and his hand found his gun.

Rommond rattled off orders over the intercom, primarily to Boulder, who was on route to the bow of the submarine, where the other ballast tanks were housed. A heave and a pant was the only response he got, but to Rommond it was confirmation enough.

"I can't do anything to get us back up, Rommond," Alson said.

"Tradam, come in," Rommond called over the intercom, but there was no response, not even a heave or a pant. The general turned to Alson. "Hold the fort."

"The fort is sinking into the moat," she said as he left the room.

Jacob sat on the floor of his quarters, gathering up the coils that had spilled from the upturned chest. Every so often the submarine tilted a little more, and the chest slid out of arm's reach. On one occasion it almost slid out the door, as if it were trying to leave the ship. There were a lot of coils to put back in their box—one of the few problems of wealth.

"When I was younger," Whistler said, as he stood by the door with his arms folded, "I had less toys in my toy box."

"Blame your mother then," Jacob replied. "Or ask Rommond for some of his."

Whistler knelt down and helped Jacob gather up the coils. He threw one or two at Jacob, who huffed in response.

"What's this?" Whistler asked, picking up a slightly brighter coil, which had a somewhat different design. He could not quite make out what it depicted, but it was clear that it was not the Iron Emperor.

"A lucky coil, perhaps," Jacob postulated. He stopped smiling when he saw Whistler's worried face. "What is it?"

Whistler pointed to the window, and his hand trembled. "There's something out there."

In the black abyss, there were creatures that even demons feared. No one knew what they looked like, not even themselves, for they were blind, and though many were scavengers, seizing and consuming any stray bits of food that had sunk down from the higher levels, there were predators too, just waiting for larger prey.

As the inhabitants of the Lifemaker dusted themselves off from their descent, and as the crew worked to get it back afloat, a great sea serpent, ten times the length of the submarine, slithered through the silt, feeling its way towards whatever had caused such a tremendous shudder on the ocean bed.

The abyss was awake, and its entire population was stirring, some to flee, some to investigate, but many, all too many, to feed. Fishes with fangs came. Bulbous bloated creatures came. Shelled monsters with massive jaws came. Things that defied description came. Every form or shape that stalked the nightmares of a child lurked there in the deep, and they all descended on the Lifemaker, no eyes to see, but many mouths to taste.

Jacob stood up slowly and turned towards the window. He felt his heart pumping like a piston, his lungs like little ballast tanks of their own. Every tiny movement was magnified, every sound amplified. The sweat dripped from his hands, forming another sea upon the floor.

Perhaps it was because of the overwhelming darkness outside, which seemed darker even than when his submersible light went out, or perhaps it was due to the look on Whistler's face, where the boy's features seemed to flee into every recess, hide behind every ridge—but Jacob knew that something evil, something hungry, was outside.

"Don't move," he whispered to Whistler. He did not think that the creature might be blind, and that he would have been better off saying: *Don't make a sound*—or saying nothing at all.

Something pressed against the window, nudging the submarine. Its hide was almost as dark as the waters around it, but its scales glistened from the light inside the room. Jacob badly wanted to douse the oil lamp, to hide inside a different darkness, but he had a feeling that any change inside the room, any step, any dimming of a light, any sound, might be like a beacon to the beast outside.

"Jacob," Whistler whispered, stammering the syllables of his name. Jacob turned slowly to him, and he saw the boy trembling so much that he might as well be moving back and forth across the room. The terror in his eyes was as though it were his nightmare that pressed against the hull. *The unknown*, Jacob thought. It was his own nightmare too.

Then, with a suddenness that seized them both, two large yellow eyes opened at the window, followed by a monstrous set of ten-inch long pointed teeth, hundreds in number. They gleamed in the light that emanated from the room, and they stabbed and slashed at the window. Though it was made of the strongest glass, so strong that it could take the increasing pressure of the ocean's greatest depths, it strained beneath the assault, and when it was not strained, it was scraped, and when it was not scraped, it cracked.

Jacob and Whistler fled as if fear itself had manifested outside. They tripped and tumbled, but they did not care, so long as they fell forwards and away from that horrid creature that tried to feed upon the glass. They ran down the corridor, and they heard shouts and screams from many of the other cabins, and dozens more people raced out from their rooms, leaving wide the doors, from which could be seen many more of the yellow-eyed, many-toothed monsters, trying to get inside.

More people joined the throng, and no one really knew where they were running to. If there were any crewmen trying to get through to the lower chambers, or trying to get to the battlements, they would have been swept up in the stampede. Some of the soldiers fled voluntarily, for though they were used to fighting demons, they had not seen anything as demonic as the creatures outside.

Jacob pulled Whistler to the side just as the mob grew so large and so loud that it almost announced itself as the greatest meal available to whatever could reach its jaws inside. Whistler narrowly avoided being trampled, for the courage of many men and women gave way to the primal lust for life. Bravery was trampled by terror, and with it went anyone who was too short, or too slow, or not strong enough, or not violent enough. Panic pierced the minds of almost everyone present, and logic was pummelled into the floor, and human decency was discarded like bait for the frightful fishes that flocked towards the submarine.

Whistler clung to Jacob, and Jacob shielded him from the storm of boots and fists, even as he shielded himself inside a doorway. The mania of his comrades helped quell his fear of monsters, and made him fear instead those same companions. The thunderous throng passed, and Jacob pulled Whistler along with him as he tried to find a way down to the lower levels.

As they ran, and as the mob's rumble faded away, they began to hear again the bashing against the windows, and the straining, cracking glass. The sounds mingled with Jacob's thoughts and gave birth to a new fear inside his heart: that if the glass broke, they would be dead long before the creatures could get close to them. No one, not even the demons of the Regime, could survive at the immense pressures of the abyss, and even if they could, they would likely drown before they set eyes upon the gaping maws of the denizens of the deep.

Down they went, echoing the descent of their vessel, into the very bowels of the ship, to save themselves from entering the bowels of something else. Jacob could feel Whistler's hand quiver in his own, and perhaps Whistler felt the reverse. The boy was such a frail thing, and yet Jacob dragged him along, and even when he tried to let go of Whistler's hand, Whistler held on tight.

They climbed down a ladder into a dark room. Jacob did not know where they were going, but this was a comforting darkness, where no yellow eyes or white fangs lit up. They stopped to catch their breath, and found that there were many breaths to catch. They heard so many sounds above, scrapes and clangs, bangs and roars. It was as if Rommond had declared war, and everyone was fighting on their own side.

Yet no matter how much the people behaved like beasts, the real assault came from the creatures outside.

Something bashed against the submarine with such a tremendous force that the vessel rocked violently from side to side, throwing people back and forth. Jacob and Whistler were not ready for the first of these, and they earned bruises as their medals, but the second time the creature shook the ship, they clung to pipes that rattled in their holdings, as if they themselves feared the larger beast that came to feast upon them all. When the vessel swung from side to side, Jacob and Whistler earned strained muscles, and then they earned an ever so brief respite, for the assailant came time and time again, and their grips grew weaker with each tumble.

Then Jacob perked his ears and heard what sounded like the firing of torpedoes from the stern. *About time*, he thought, though he dared not think of the trouble those crewmen had with arming those weapons, nor of those panicked people who had abandoned their posts. He looked at Whistler and forced a reassuring smile.

"We're fighting back," he said. He wished he could fight as well.

Taberah and Alakovi led the counter-assault, loading and firing torpedoes as if there was an unlimited supply. There was not.

Neither of the women had any love for the other, but they both had hate in abundance for their assailant, and though they could not see it, they knew it in their hearts that it was just one massive and mighty creature that lunged itself against the submarine.

Alakovi hauled up the massive torpedo shells and loaded them into the torpedo bays, and Taberah fired them as soon as the hatch banged shut. Other soldiers and volunteers from both the Resistance and the Order loaded other torpedoes, though never as quickly as this female pair.

Though they could not see, and they feared to turn on the many bright lights of the submarine, in case they might attract more foul beasts, they heard the cries of the gargantuan creature as missiles struck its hulking form. At times the explosions forced the monster to retreat, but other times they made it attack with greater ferocity.

They knew it was big, and they knew it was angry. What they did not know was that now it was wrapping its serpentine form around the entire hull—and preparing to squeeze.

The submarine stopped rocking, and Jacob let go of the pipes. Whistler was reluctant to let go of his, but he was even more reluctant to be left behind as Jacob climbed back up the ladder to their deck.

"It looks like the worst is over," Jacob said, as if to tempt fate. "Maybe we should find Rommond," Whistler suggested.

"He's probably outside," Jacob said, "bare-knuckle boxing with the beast."

As amusing as this thought was to Jacob, it did little to cheer Whistler. "I think there's still something out there."

They found their way into one of the armouries, which was loaded with pistols and rifles, useful only for a battle inside the submarine. They looked through the supplies, but there were no torpedoes or harpoons, and no real way to fire them.

Then they heard a series of creaking and grinding noises, and they saw the hull begin to buckle. It was not from the pressure of the ocean depths, but from the monstrous serpent that wound its way around the submarine, constricting the metal, choking the steel.

Jacob and Whistler backed away from the crinkling metal walls, but there was nowhere truly to run, for everywhere they went, the walls warped around them. They knew that if the hull did not breach, where death would wash in upon them all, it was only a matter of time before everyone was crushed inside.

"Back to your stations," Rommond called calmly over the intercom, as if being crushed inside a metal cylinder was an everyday occurrence. "All hands, turn on every light. Repeat, all hands, turn on every light."

Even from this vantage point, Jacob and Whistler could see the water outside illuminating from the powerful spotlights around the ship.

"What is he doing?" Jacob said. He meant to just think it.

Whistler raised his hand. "I think he's trying to scare them away."

The light went on in Jacob's mind. In a world of darkness, the only real weapon was the light.

Jacob and Whistler ran from room to room, turning on or turning up every light they could find. They split up to gain speed, purpose conquering panic, duty quelling fear. It seemed that every gaslight and oil lamp was not quite bright enough, and many were bits of broken metal and glass on the floor, and some were completely starved of fuel. Others joined the frantic illumination of the vessel, finding battery-powered torches and shining them out the windows. In time, the submarine was a solitary lighthouse on the ocean floor.

The sea serpent was not completely blind, but it took every light imaginable to penetrate its weak eyes. When they did, especially the powerful spotlights, which scattered many of the other ugly fishes that came close enough to their rays, the snake let go of the ship and issued a horrendous howl that rocked the ocean depths. It wriggled away, sending up silt and weeds in its wake, and leaving the Lifemaker for some other more daring predator.

Nothing else attacked the submarine that day, or the days that followed, but every sound was heard as the battle cry of a beast, every creak the war song of the deep. Nerves were frayed, and many among the crew found it difficult to rest, and impossible to sleep. For those who fought their way into the realms of slumber, the battle raged on in their dreams.

Immediately after the attack, Alson insisted over the intercom that the worst was over, but it was clear to everyone that the submarine still was not rising. The light might have been scaring away the creatures of the dark, but that light could not hold out forever. Nor, indeed, could the ship's oxygen supply.

Rommond marched down to the lower levels, where Jacob and Whistler lurked in the shadows. The smuggler hid there from the prying light, and yet still felt like he was being watched. Whistler would have preferred to stay out of the darkness, but not if it meant staying out of it alone.

"You," Rommond said, almost seizing Jacob with the word, as if it were a spell. "Come with me." The general walked off before awaiting a response. It seemed as if he did not even want a *Yes, sir*. He wanted action.

Jacob was surprised at how quickly he sprang into motion, like a good little soldier. He was not sure if it was the urgency in Rommond's voice that made him go, or if it was the fact that he felt safer in the general's company. Whistler trotted along behind them.

"Not you, Brogan," the general said, without stopping or turning.

"But I—"

"Not you."

Whistler halted and shrunk his shoulders. Jacob turned to him and shrugged, trying to convey *What can I do?* It was not exactly like he had much sway with the general. He also had a feeling that Rommond was going somewhere he deemed dangerous, which was why he did not want the boy along. Jacob, on the other hand, was expendable. All smugglers were.

"You look like a man on a mission," Jacob said, trying hard to keep up with Rommond's long and even strides.

"I am."

"Where are we going?"

"To solve a mystery."

"I love a good mystery," Jacob said with a smile.

"I don't."

They continued on until they came to the aft ballast room, which was darker than most other places on the submarine. Jacob mused that perhaps that was why Rommond wanted him to accompany him. Perhaps he thought that he could see better in the dark.

"Help me with these," Rommond said, handing rubber tubing to Jacob.

"What do I attach this with?"

"You're standing on them."

Jacob stepped aside to find several hexagon nuts on the floor. He picked them up and began fastening them into place.

"You sure we want to use these if they came loose before?" Jacob asked.

Rommond stared at him in the darkness. "They didn't come loose."

They reconnected the cannisters of compressed air to the ballast tanks and sealed them tight.

"We're good at the stern," Rommond called over the intercom.

"A few minutes more at the bow," Boulder panted back. Jacob imagined the head mechanic rolling back and forth at the forward ballast tanks, causing more damage.

"Bring us up quick," Rommond called to Alson over the intercom.

He did not need to, as the submarine already began to rise. It shuddered as more of the smaller sea creatures attacked it, and it sank a little as barnacle beasts attached themselves to the hull like leaden weights. As soon as Boulder's work was complete, however, it rose swiftly, leaving the black abyss, and its blind inhabitants, for the slightly paler black of the level above.

"Well, that was fun," Jacob said.

Rommond scoffed. "You have a strange idea of fun."

"I knew a girl who would have loved all this excitement."

"I'm jolly glad she isn't with you still," Rommond said. He began to carefully patrol between the tanks, as if one of them might suddenly come alive.

"What are we looking for?" Jacob asked as he

strolled along behind him.

Again Rommond did not respond. He stopped when he bumped his foot against a wrench on the floor. He picked it up and held it to the light.

"Boulder is not this sloppy," Rommond said.

He could have fooled me, Jacob thought. He almost said it too.

Rommond continued on, clutching the wrench tightly in his hand. For a moment he almost looked like a murderer, stalking his prey. The shadow he cast on the wall was sinister. Jacob trailed a little further behind than before.

"We could do with better lights in here," Rommond said.

"We could do with better lights everywhere," Jacob suggested.

He banged his elbow against one of the tanks, as if to prove the point. He grimaced, and Rommond turned to him sharply, wrench at the ready, before resuming his careful patrol. Jacob followed slowly, nursing the wound.

Rommond grabbed the oil lamp in the centre of the room and held it before him. The light attacked the darkness, sending it fleeing into the corners. It also attacked their eyes, and it made the shadows look a little bit like attackers of their own.

Where's my wrench? Jacob thought. He noticed his hands were clenched into fists. He was not sure if he was trying to steady the tremors or prepare for a fight.

They reached one of the furthest corners of the room, where the shadows conspired. A darker shape was there in the gloom, lying still. Jacob squinted in the darkness. He thought it almost looked like a boot.

Rommond shone the lamp at the shape, and the shadows fled from the body it revealed. Even in the darkness, Jacob could see the pool of blood around it.

Rommond reached down and turned the body over, revealing the Resistance uniform. There was no doubt who it was. Tradam was dead, and his gun was missing.

"Hell," Jacob said. He hoped he was not condemning the man.

Rommond took out his pistol. "We have a saboteur on board."

Chapter Fourteen

INTERROGATION

Rommond convened a hasty meeting between his top advisers, and it was a great surprise to Jacob to find himself invited. He was less surprised when he found himself the focus of many of the questions. It was not long before it started to look like an interrogation.

"What happened after the incident with Teller?" Rommond asked.

"What do you mean?" Jacob asked in turn.

"Was he killed?"

"I don't really—"

"Did he die? Did he fall to tribal darts? Did you shoot him?"

"I didn't kill him. I was kind of trying to stop being killed myself. Me and Whistler just ran for it."

"Ran for what?"

"For our lives."

"So Teller might still be alive."

"I suppose so, yeah."

Rommond turned to his fellow commanders with a grave expression. They looked to each other, as if they had discussed this possibility before.

"What's with the interrogation?" Jacob asked.

"Why didn't you ask me all this before?"

"It wasn't important before."

"Do you actually think Teller is on board? Wouldn't we have encountered him by now?"

"It's a big ship," Taberah said.

"Hell, he'd leave a trail of slime," Jacob said, "like a snail."

"A trail that no one seemed to notice before," Rommond grumbled. He looked to Taberah. "I told you he couldn't be trusted."

"You said that about a lot of people, people we now rely on," Taberah replied. "Mudro. Boulder. Karlsif. All people you had doubts about at first. I can't just discard people left, right and centre when we need them."

"What about when you don't need them?" Jacob asked.

Taberah looked at him, but did not reply.

"We haven't confirmed that Teller is eliminated," Rommond said. "He wormed his way in once before, while we were looking, so who knows if he has wormed his way in again, when we weren't looking." He turned to Taberah. "Are you sure you weren't followed when you rescued Jacob and the boy?"

Taberah looked insulted. "It's the Silver Ghost, Rommond."

"It's not the Invisible Ghost. Silver can still be seen in the desert."

"I wasn't followed."

"Did you take a winding way to Dustdelving after you picked them up?"

Jacob watched Taberah closely as her agitation

rose. *Your turn to be interrogated*. He was surprised when she did not answer the general's question.

"Did you take a winding path?" Rommond asked again, a little sterner.

"I didn't see the need," Taberah said after another pause. She clearly would have preferred silence as her answer. To Jacob, and likely the general, that still would have said a lot.

Rommond was livid. "You didn't see the need?" he quizzed. He turned left and right, where his commanders pursed their lips, as if afraid to speak. Rommond leaned back in his chair and interlocked his fingers, as if to stop them grabbing his gun.

"We were evacuating," Taberah explained.

"Because they had a good idea where we were," Rommond said. "They didn't know exactly where we were."

"What would it have mattered? We were getting out of there."

"They didn't know we had the Lifemaker," the general said. If it had been anyone else, they would have shouted it; instead, his pitch was slightly higher, and significantly sterner. "Anyone could have followed you. Anyone could have seen us packing up shop and setting sail."

"Anyone could have got on board," Jacob interjected.

Rommond gestured towards Jacob. "*Anyone could have got on board*."

"We would have seen them," Taberah said.

"Did you see everyone who came on board?" the general asked.

"No," she replied. "But I'm not the ship's security."

"So you're going to put this lapse on *my* men?"

"Rommond, you're making assumptions about Teller."

"You mean, like I made when you first introduced him to me?"

"That he's still alive," she said, gritting her teeth.

"I hope to all gods that he's not," Rommond said, "and if he is, I'll kill him myself. But the big issue here is that you went against protocol. You didn't follow instruction. I notice this is a habit of yours. A dangerous habit, Taberah."

"It was *Resistance* protocol," Taberah said. "The Order has different rules."

"Like letting spies in."

"I seem to recall that Daniel was one of *your* men before he joined the Order," Taberah said.

"Don't put Brogan's capture on me, Taberah. You're careless with your group. You can't just run in to every situation guns blazing."

"You can't just sit back and wait for things to get better either," she replied. "Things aren't going to go back to the way they were. We're not fighting for the past, Rommond. We're fighting for the future."

"I *know* what we're fighting for."

"Then stop criticising me for giving my all for it."

"It's not your all that I'm worried about. It's the fact that while you're giving your all, you're risking people's lives."

"If I risk them by doing something, you risk them by doing nothing."

"Doing nothing? Do you think that all of this,

this ship, all these plans, is doing nothing?"

"You can plan to the ends of the universe. We need action."

"We need careful, planned action."

"Planning didn't save Brooklyn, did it?"

Rommond stood up sharply. "Get out."

Taberah waited for a moment, returning Rommond's glare with her own. Then she left the room, and the meeting was quickly ended. Jacob heard many people condemning Taberah, some for her current words, and some for her past actions. Everyone had an opinion on her. Few were good.

Rommond ordered small units of soldiers to search every level for an intruder, of which they found no sign, and he posted guards at the entrances and exits of every deck, and swapped them regularly. Whenever these were encountered, it reminded the workers that while the monsters of the abyss were no longer a threat, there might still be a monster on board.

"She's got a big mouth," Mudro said, drawing up beside Jacob as he left the room. "No wonder the boy can't keep his closed either. Learned it from her, sure didn't he?"

"Sometimes it's best to keep it bolted shut," Jacob said. *Not that I've been any good at that.*

"The pipe's good for that. If you're smoking, you're not talking."

"Maybe I'll take it up."

"The problem is the limited supply of leaf," the doctor said.

It's limited because you keep using it all up, Jacob thought. "Best to keep it for the sick then," he said. He thought of Whistler, who had not needed the pain-killing leaf for over a month, but who still needed bandages on the burns.

"She had the audacity to name me," Mudro grumbled. "It took a long time for Rommond to trust me, and longer to get into his inner circle. I don't need her raising more doubts about me in his mind."

"Why did you join the Order?" Jacob asked. "Did you not feel like you were betraying Rommond?"

"I felt like it, sure, but he was in a bad state at the time. It was just after the whole Brooklyn disaster. He was a lot more daring with his tactics before. Then he didn't want to risk anything that looked too dangerous on paper, anything that might get people killed. He blamed himself, of course. There isn't any magic to make blame go away, that's for sure. We all stuck with him for a time, but many of us became restless. The Regime was winning new ground, reclaiming land we'd taken with Rommond's previous pushes. Taberah wanted to act, and there were a good few of us who felt the same."

"Is that when the coup happened?"

Mudro chuckled. "It wasn't a coup."

"You're the second person who's said that. It kind of sounds like a coup to me."

"We didn't want Rommond out. We wanted a change in direction. Taberah started asking around for support for a leadership challenge. Word got back to Rommond quick, probably from the Copper Matron. She was always very protective of him.

And boy did he act quick then. We all thought Taberah was done for. We didn't exactly feel secure ourselves. But Rommond came up with a solution, a compromise for it all. He handed over the amulet side of the Resistance to Taberah, since it was an area she'd focused on so much before, and he let her take anyone who was willing to go with her. I'm not sure if he knew it, if he was just that confident, but not many of us left. Most of our crew are new recruits, and it was hard to get them. We'd take anyone."

"That's where I come in," Jacob said.

"And Teller."

"And him."

"Really it's just Taberah, Soasa, and myself left of the old guard. We had a few more from the Resistance in the early days, and a handful more that joined over time, but we lost most of them."

"From Taberah's carelessness?"

"A bit of that. But as Taberah would say, *they knew what they signed up for*. If they wanted the careful approach, they'd have stuck with Rommond."

"I imagine it hurt though," Jacob said. "I mean, for Rommond."

"I've no doubt it did. Taberah and he were very close. They worked together from very early on. Sure, they were there for the Glassfinder Project, which was before I got involved. After the so-called 'coup,' relations were strained for a good six months, but they met frequently to discuss 'the bigger picture,' as they often put it. Didn't take long before they were discussing the little picture as well. They were either going to be the best of friends or the worst of enemies.

I can't see there being a middle ground with them."

"So what about what happened back there? Do you think that'll strain things?"

Mudro halted suddenly, and waved his pipe in the air, leaving behind a trail of smoke that took the shape of a heart. He drove the pipe down quickly between it, severing it in two. "There's one sure way to make a friendship with Rommond disappear," he said. "And that's to say anything bad about Brooklyn."

Chapter Fifteen

REST AND REPAIRS

There was still some life left in the Lifemaker, but it had taken a battering. Boulder might have been a lot thinner from all the running back and forth, plugging leaks, tapping out dints, and connecting bits and bobs that had come unscrewed—were it not for all the beer he guzzled along the way. Jacob could not blame him, and had plenty of sips of his own. *Calm the nerves*, he thought. Boulder looked as though he could have done with a lot more calming.

But he was not the only grease monkey swinging back and forth through the metal jungle, for Alakovi had the Copper Vixens out in force, focusing less on the army of vehicles housed in the lower levels, which was their primary responsibility, and more on that one vehicle they all depended on so much. The women toiled with tools as if it were second nature to them, and Taberah and Soasa did their part, albeit always out of eyeline and earshot of their old sorority sisters.

Jacob did his bit too, and he never worked so hard, tightening bolts, putting back up doors, sealing cracks in the windows, reinforcing the hull, and tending to any other of the submarine's many ailments. As soon as one thing was fixed, it seemed that another problem announced itself, and there were not enough men and women for all the faults. Whistler made every effort to help, though it was often too much for him just to haul the toolbox from job to job.

"I hope we're getting paid for this," Jacob shouted over to Boulder on one of his many trips by. Jacob stuck his tongue out at Whistler, who was rolling his eyes at the comment.

"Oh, you better ask the big guy," Boulder said, taking it all very seriously. His hair and thick sideburns were plastered in sweat. "But let me tell you this, laddie," he added, and he pulled Jacob close enough to smell the alcohol on his breath, "he'll likely tell you that you're gettin' paid with your continued breath o' life."

Alakovi was a rare sight, but she was heard well before she was seen. On one occasion she thundered through, ignoring all questions or comments, on a mission to murder whatever problem she was tasked with. It was abundantly clear that she was unhappy with being dragged away from work on Rommond's other vehicles.

It was a long time before Rommond patrolled the levels to inspect the work, and here and there make a tiny adjustment of his own when something did not quite look, in his words, "bang on." Before that, he rounded up anyone known to have deserted his or her post, and gave them a right telling off, and threatened to send them out the airlocks, and reminded them of their oaths and obligations, and then gave them twice as much work to do as anyone else in repairing the ship.

The general was, therefore, in a grim mood when he came around to inspect Jacob's work. He stopped for a long time and said nothing, and he glanced back and forth at Jacob and Whistler, and at the repairs they had managed.

"Hmm," he managed, with great effort.

"Is that a *You've done a wonderful job* kind of *Hmm*?" Jacob asked.

"Perhaps."

"A perfect job?" Jacob wondered, putting his arm around Whistler's shoulder and posing proudly beside the pipework the two had just reassembled.

"Not quite," Rommond said. He put on one of his gloves and twisted one of the pipes a millimetre to the left.

Jacob chuckled. "That was fine the way it was."

"Fine, perhaps, but not perfect," the general said. "My motto, or one of them anyway, is: *'Good enough' is not good enough.*"

Jacob smiled. "And mine is: *Spend all day on these pipes and nothing else gets done.*"

"Fair enough, Jacob. You're doing a … *fine* … job." Rommond turned to Whistler. "And you, young chap, you've done a bang up job here. Very well done!"

Whistler beamed and looked to his feet, as if the attention was too much for him.

"And you're looking much better too," the general continued. "Give Mudro my regards!"

Rommond passed on quickly to the next lot of workers, and Jacob and Whistler turned to their next task. It was strenuous work, and very few people were not employed for it, and those that were not, such as the majority of the pregnant women, made and brought around sandwiches for the toiling labourers. As back-breaking as the work was, most were glad to do it, for it distracted them from the horrors of the abyss.

Several days into the repairs, Jacob and Whistler's route brought them in touch with Taberah, who was working alone.

"Should you really be doing any of this?" Jacob asked. "It's, what, two months in?"

"I'm not an invalid," she barked at him.

"I didn't say you were. I'm just wondering if it's good for the baby."

"If we don't get this submarine fixed up, that won't be good for the baby either."

"Okay, okay. Well, where's Soasa? I thought she was supposed to be helping you?"

"I sent her away," Taberah stated. "She was starting to annoy me."

"I guess she has that effect on people," Jacob acknowledged.

Taberah raised an eyebrow. "So do you."

Jacob grinned and cast a devilish glance at his co-conspirator Whistler, who appeared to be less comfortable in Taberah's company than in Jacob's. The boy looked to the floor throughout the entire exchange, saying nothing.

"Rommond gave you a hard time in there," Jacob said to Taberah.

"I probably deserve it," she replied.

"I was hoping it wasn't going to come to blows."

Taberah's eyes were grim. "There's time yet for that."

"You probably shouldn't have mentioned Brooklyn."

"He needs to get over that. It's holding him back. It's holding all of us back."

"That may be true," Jacob said, "but it's not easy to let go of the past. Would you be able to do it if you were in his boots?"

"It's funny how you've suddenly become his ally," Taberah said.

"It's not about—"

"Let me get back to work, Jacob."

He complied, leading Whistler away as Taberah took her anger out on the ship. She might have captured him in her web, but it seemed to him that she was destroying the threads that held it up, and held her up too.

Chapter Sixteen

SURVIVAL

The nights on the Lifemaker were the worst, if anyone could truly tell that it was night; the waters outside the windows remained dark for every hour of the day. They were two months into their journey by now, and Taberah was feeling restless.

Often she paced through the submarine in the small hours of the night, when her mind raced endlessly, robbing her of sleep. She knew that Rommond was up, sitting in his library alone, but she did not disturb him. She suspected that Jacob was up as well, exploring the vessel. Rommond sat and brooded, Jacob strolled, and Taberah paced.

She found Marya on a lower deck, just above the forbidden floor, also pacing.

"Maybe our unborn children need the exercise," Taberah said to the young woman, startling her.

"I guess," Marya said. "I couldn't sleep."

"I never sleep nowadays, it seems," Taberah said.

"The baby … it makes it tough," Marya said.

Taberah nodded, but did not speak.

"I don't think I want to go through with this," Marya revealed, when the silence let her stew in her own thoughts. "The pregnancy, I mean. I'm not sure I can go through with it."

"You have to," Taberah stated.

"What do you mean?"

"You really don't have a choice."

"But I—"

"But nothing. We need to continue our species. This is duty."

Marya slumped her head and shoulders, and said nothing.

"Do you think I want this?" Taberah asked. "I don't *want* another child. Yet for years I've kept trying. Man after man. And you know what? As much as a part of me hoped each time to get pregnant, another part hoped against it. Because what good would I be as leader of the Order if I could barely walk or stand without aches, always worrying that I could lose the child at any moment, or lose what makes me … me. Really, what does a child make me?"

Marya thought on this long and hard. "More of a woman, I guess." It did not seem she entirely believed it.

Taberah scoffed. "And less of a warrior."

"Why do you want to *be* a warrior?"

"I don't," Taberah said, "but we are at war. We need everyone to fight, in their own way."

"But why *this* way?"

"You have to think of the bigger picture, Marya. Our little pains and discomforts are nothing against what we're trying to achieve. People like Jacob focus on the little things, the meaningless things, but it's the bigger picture that matters. A few lives here and there are insignificant. It's the fate of humanity as a whole that's at stake. Can't you see that?"

"I can," Marya said, "but why … why does it have to be me? Can't someone else bear that burden?"

Taberah did not feign sympathy. "Why do you, one of the Pure, have to continue the bloodline of our people? I don't know, Marya. Why did thousands of soldiers die in the trenches trying to save our people? Why did so many people lose the ones they love? Why do we face extinction? Why did the demons come in the first place?"

"I guess I don't really have a reason for self-pity," Marya said, looking more disheartened than ever. "We have to stop asking *Why?* and start asking *What now?*" Taberah continued. "This is the world we live in. What now can we do about it?"

"I guess I can carry on."

"It's the least you can do."

"Some of the other women seem to like being pregnant."

"Good," Taberah said. "It'll make it easier for them to fulfil their duty."

"And love their children."

"Sure," Taberah said. "So long as they have the children in the first place." She paused for a moment while they walked, feeling the baby that was growing inside her. "We need lives, not love."

Chapter Seventeen

THE FORBIDDEN FLOOR

The Lifemaker was in good shape, but the repairs were ongoing. Jacob thought this was the perfect opportunity to take a look at the forbidden floor. Had Rommond not refused him access, he might have felt less inclined to investigate. He wanted to know what the general was creating down there, what the Copper Vixens were forging in the hidden ironworks. He had seen some of the vessels when he first boarded, but that level was quickly sealed off from his frequent wanderings.

Whistler was much more reluctant to explore the forbidden deck, despite his immense curiosity, which was greater than Jacob's. It was only his respect and admiration for Rommond, which was also greater than Jacob's, that kept him from rummaging about in the general's toy-box. When Jacob stated emphatically that he was going down there anyway, and two could hardly cause any more trouble than one, Whistler's adventurous side quickly got the better of him. That was the thing about adventure—it did not take much convincing. *A little mischief never did anyone any harm.* At least that's what he told Whistler.

* * *

The constant coming and going of crewmen working on repairs helped the duo easily bypass the guards that Rommond had put in place. No one really knew who was authorised to do what, and many of the soldiers were looking out for someone that fitted Teller's description. If Teller really was aboard the vessel, Jacob thought that he was unlikely to show his slimy face now that the alarm had been raised.

It did not take long for Jacob to find the Hopebreaker in the chambers below, sparkling clean as if it had never seen a desert storm. There was not a dint or scratch on the plaque at the back of the vehicle that bore its name. "Mint condition" was clearly another of Rommond's catchphrases.

"I wonder if he'll mind if I take it for a spin," Jacob said.

"He'll mind!" Whistler replied. He frantically followed Jacob around, rubbing his sleeve over any part of the landship that Jacob touched, polishing away the fingerprints.

"I have a feeling I'd just—" Jacob paused and held up a piece of grating that had come loose in his hand. "Well, more than a feeling then." He placed the grating back delicately. "Shoddy workmanship if you ask me."

"He'll kill you!" Whistler exclaimed. "He'll kill both of us!"

"It probably came loose in the abyss. Those strange fishes did it."

"They didn't leave your fingerprints," Whistler said as he began vigorously cleaning the grating.

* * *

They skulked about some more, but were soon spotted.

"You," the Copper Matron called out. "You shouldn't be down here."

Jacob froze, and Whistler hid in the shadows behind him. Jacob turned around slowly. "Is this off-limits?" he asked innocently.

"You bet your ass it is," Alakovi blurted, "and don't you be thinkin' I don't know *all* about you."

"I don't know what you mean," Jacob protested. "I was just looking for the loo."

"There's a giant one all around the ship!"

"It's a bit hard to reach," Jacob said, rapping his knuckles on the metal hull.

"I'll get Boulder to let you know the next time we have a leak!"

"Much appreciated," Jacob said as he tried to slink away.

"Where d'you think you're off to?"

"The loo," Jacob said.

"And what, d'you need two of you for that?"

Whistler came out from behind Jacob, his hands in his pockets, his shoulders raised, and his eyes held low.

"Your mother'd be ashamed of you! And you should be ashamed of her!"

"All right, lesson learned," Jacob said. "We'll stay out of your hair."

"It's not me hair I'm worried about," the mechanic roared. "Stay out o' the ironworks!"

"And where is that?" Jacob asked with a grin.

Alakovi almost had a fit. "Wh-where is that?" she

shouted, almost choking on her breath, as if the very machinery had rebelled against her. "Why, it's this entire bloody level! And they say I'm blind! Oh, I've seen you skulking about in the shadows down here before."

"I haven't been down here before," Jacob said.

"You can't pull the wool over my eyes, smuggler. I spotted you!"

"Well, now that we know where the ironworks is," Jacob said, "we'll be sure to avoid it."

He turned and pushed Whistler ahead, who seemed like he would have stayed for the entire telling off. Jacob did not need to hear the rest. He had heard enough of them before.

"You're a bad influence, you are!" the Copper Matron shouted after him, shaking a spanner in the air as if she thought a few thumps of that might have been a better influence.

Whistler broke into a giggle when they were out of view and earshot of the raging mechanic. Given how despondent Whistler had seemed before, Jacob thought that he was just the influence the kid needed.

Not all the workers of the lower levels were displeased to see the explorers from the world of the decks above. Some had not seen other people from those levels in days, others in weeks. Some had only heard of Rommond by name, and to a handful of them he was as mythical as the Iron Emperor himself. They toiled inside the toy-box, creating the many wondrous machines the Resistance had used previously, and those even more wonderful, and dangerous, ones it planned to use in the future.

They stayed out of the Matron's way, hiding in the shadows, watching the workers assemble and maintain a vast array of vehicles. Among them the Hopebreaker stood out prominently, and it received significant attention from Alakovi, as if it was as much her baby as it was Rommond's.

Something that held Whistler's attention more than any other was an airship, which was still under construction. The balloon itself was deflated, but the carriage was colossal and ornate, much like many of Rommond's prized possessions. Jacob was a little amused by Whistler's gawking reaction to this marvel of the skies.

"Let me guess," Jacob said, "you want to fly."

"Who doesn't?"

"I can take it or leave it."

"But you get to soar above the world, like an eagle."

"And still all you see is desert."

"And all those fluffy clouds," Whistler said wistfully.

Jacob stopped himself from sharing any more of his personal cynicism, in case it would deflate the balloon of the boy's hopes and dreams. Just because his own wings were burnt, it did not mean he had to burn others'. "It must be fun though," he said. "Hell, it's got to beat hiding beneath the waves."

They explored the forbidden floor further, keeping mostly to the shadows. The numerous vehicles afforded plenty of cover, and the constant bang of hammers and other tools masked their footsteps and voices. Before long they found themselves at the stern of the ship, deep beneath where the aft ballast tanks were stored. The darkness there was more oppressing.

"I think I've found something," Whistler called out. Jacob barely made it over before he saw Whistler plummet through a hole in the floor. He tried to grab him, but the boy was already deep below. He heard the painful thud of the body, and Whistler's groans.

"Are you okay?" Jacob shouted down. He realised that perhaps shouting was not the best idea.

"Ow," Whistler replied.

"Are you all right?" Jacob asked.

"Kind of," Whistler said. "Yes. I just … there's something down here."

An image of a monstrous creature or the rumoured saboteur flashed in Jacob's mind. He leapt down the opening to fight it, giving his own groans as he struck the floor several metres below. But there was no creature or person there besides him and Whistler.

"Thought you'd have a better look?" Whistler asked.

"Of course," Jacob said, lowering his fighting stance.

"Well, look at this." Whistler rubbed his hand across a dust-covered door, removing some of the grime that obscured a strange symbol.

"What is that, a flower?" Jacob asked.

"I think it's supposed to be a fire."

Jacob saw it now. It was eight interlocking flames,

spaced around a circle, with the points outwards.

"I'm not sure we should be here," Whistler said.

Jacob tapped his knuckles on the iron door. "I've got to know what's in there now."

Chapter Eighteen

THE IRON DOOR

The most interesting part of the forbidden floor was no longer the marvellous machinery, but rather the mysterious black door with its many rivets and its arcane symbol. It was a barrier which would not budge, and which stood like a sentinel, guarding some secret treasure inside.

Whistler nicknamed it the Iron Door, after the Iron Wall that skirted the Regime's primary domain. The latter was a train track that ran from north to south, and on it was the largest and fastest rail gun the world of Altadas had ever known. The Resistance had lost many men and machines against that monster, and so the legend grew that the Iron Wall could not be penetrated. Though Whistler's appellation for this latest boundary might have been apt, it did not stop them from trying.

Jacob procured a crowbar, which proved useless against the door, which had been sealed so tightly it might as well have been welded shut. Eventually Jacob proposed that it was a false door, part of the wall crafted purely for design. This greatly disappointed Whistler, who was not entirely convinced. Jacob was certain the door was real, and though his curiosity was great, he could not help but think: *What terrible thing could be behind that door, for them to lock it so tight?*

They abandoned this fruitless quest, and climbed back up into the ironworks, and crept out of the forbidden deck without Alakovi or the guards noticing them. Work went on, more repairs were made, and the mischievous duo looked to other things to pass the time.

Two days passed since the discovery of the Iron Door, when Jacob bumped into Soasa in the corridor. She seemed to be more explosive than ever, and instead of trying to avoid the smuggler, she was actively seeking him out.

"You!" she cried, grabbing him by the collar and smacking him on the head.

"What the hell?" Jacob asked as he recoiled from her.

"If you take another stick of dynamite from my store, I'll make sure the next one is in your bed."

"I didn't take anything."

"Sure you didn't," Soasa said. "And I didn't take some of your coils as reparation."

"Soasa, I swear to you," Jacob said, holding his hands up, palms outward, "that I didn't steal any of your supplies."

"That just makes you a liar as well as a thief."

"What would I have used them for anyway?" Jacob asked.

"Don't pretend you don't know."

"Honest to God, Soasa, I haven't a clue what

you're talking about."

"The door," she said. "The one you blew open."

"What?"

"Here!" she cried, dragging him by the arm as she marched off. Whistler saw them as she neared the hatch to the forbidden floor, and he began to follow.

"What's going on?" he asked.

"Someone blew open the Iron Door," Jacob told him.

Soasa growled. "See, I knew you knew all about it!"

"I knew about the door, not the dynamite. Anyway, how did you know I knew?"

Whistler gave a sheepish grin. "Sorry," he said. "I had to tell someone about it. I thought maybe she knew a way in." He looked back and forth between Jacob and the ground, barely able to mask the look of guilt.

"You didn't blow it up, did you?" Jacob asked.

"No!" Whistler protested. "No, of course not."

"Good," the smuggler said. Though that just raised another, more worrying question: Who did?

They arrived at the Iron Door, which was blown fully open. Inside, Jacob and Whistler found a toy they hoped no one would ever play with: a colossal bomb, so big that they knew instantly that if it was ever dropped, if any city should ever be its unfortunate target, it would change the world forever.

When Rommond arrived at the site of this discovery, he had his gun in hand, while his other was a clenched fist.

"Out!" he bellowed, and he ushered all of them out of the room with the butt of the gun.

"What's this all about?" Jacob asked.

"Never you mind," the general said through gritted teeth. He looked like he could blow up at any moment, and cause just as much devastation.

"Rommond," Taberah said, "what is that thing?" Really she was asking: Why? The fact that she did not know was disconcerting to Jacob, as it likely was to many others. It seemed that very few among them knew about the bomb, and none of those were willing to speak.

"An experiment," the general said in time, "and we might as well be the guinea pigs, what with someone rigging dynamite so close to it. I want to know who did this, and I'll have the heads of anyone who hides the culprit." He glared at Jacob.

Great, Jacob thought. *Just like me to be the likely suspect.*

"You do know that Soasa's the dynamite gal, right?" Jacob said.

Soasa lunged at him, but was hauled back by several others, including Taberah. "The nerve of you!" Soasa shouted. "Those sticks were stolen, Rommond. I'm not the one skulking around the ship, searching for every shadow to hide in."

"It doesn't exactly make sense for someone who likes sneaking around to start blowing things up," Jacob said.

"Enough!" Rommond roared. It was the first time Jacob had seen him this angry. He usually managed to keep his cool. Jacob thought it was not just about the damage, but the fact that the general's dark secret, of the existence of that terrible weapon, was exposed.

"I want all of you out of here," the general continued. "And I want this sealed up tight. And by God, I want all your mouths sealed up about it too." He looked at Whistler in particular.

"Rommond," Taberah said. "What about the bomb? Are we in danger?"

"It isn't live," he replied. "And it isn't quite finished yet anyway."

"But when it is?"

"When it is," Rommond said, sighing deeply, "God help us all."

Chapter Nineteen

UNDERWATER TRADE

The Iron Door was resealed, albeit in a somewhat makeshift fashion, and everyone who had seen what was stored inside was sworn to secrecy. The Copper Vixens had their own oaths, but Rommond made it clear that anyone who spoke about the "weapon" would be sent back down to the bottom of the ocean, with leaden weights around their boots.

The mood on the Lifemaker was grim after the discovery, even though few knew about it. The knowledge was toxic, a weapon of its own, and though no one said a word, it created a deep malaise in every mind. Some begged to have their quarters moved from the stern to the bow, feeling unsafe being so close to the bomb, but all such requests were denied. If it went off, no one on the Lifemaker would be safe.

Rommond's commanders conducted interrogations of likely suspects for the explosion, attempting as best they could to keep everything "hush-hush." Jacob was asked many questions, but he also found that he was often followed, as if they believed his actions much more than they believed his words. Yet nothing came of the investigation, and Rommond was keener to keep things quiet than pursue things further. He tripled the guard for the ironworks, and he was often found patrolling the area himself. If there really was a saboteur on board, the general was intent on catching him with his own hands.

The Lifemaker rose to higher waters, partly from fear of the abyss below, but also because Rommond wanted to conduct an underwater trade. Jacob presumed that this was intended as a distraction from recent events, but Rommond insisted that the Resistance needed to acquire some final items before it started to resist a little more forcefully. Jacob hoped that those items were not parts for the bomb.

"This is how we gained supply for years," Rommond explained to Jacob, after Jacob was not content to just witness what was transpiring.

"Slipping bits and bobs right under the Regime's nose," Jacob mused. "Seems safe."

"You might even call it smuggling," Rommond replied.

They waited in the cargo bay, where a large round window showed the reassuring dark blue of those waters, about halfway between the abyss and the surface, still too deep to track, but not deep enough to be totally blind. A single light shone from the Lifemaker, illuminating a bizarre underwater vessel, which creaked slowly towards them.

It was the oddest looking contraption any of them, bar perhaps Rommond and Taberah, had seen. There were eighteen propellers, three on every side, and three on the top and bottom, and though only some of these were working at any given time, it made the submersible look bizarre. There were also visible pistons and pipes, curling around one another, tacked together and riveted to the hull in a rather slipshod manner. Fins protruded out at seemingly random intervals, and the top of the vessel was marked by a series of glass domes, some on top of the other. The hull was of many different metals, as patchwork as Whistler's clothes, and the interior was even worse, a ransack of cogs, levers and pulleys, and bits and pieces of pretty much everything that could be salvaged, taped and tacked together, and holding on and up by who knows what, bar perhaps sheer will alone.

It docked with the Lifemaker, latching into place at the primary cargo airlock. Alakovi made sure everything was in place, and her Vixens prepared a crate of coils nearby. Jacob heard the suction of rubber, the click of clamps, the release of the water, and the hiss of the air. Then the inner dock of the airlock opened, and in stepped a thin, tall man, with the strangest sense of dress, as colourful as it was crude, as mismatching as it was gaudy.

"How d'you do," the man said, his voice as clashing as his clothes; he alternated between deep rumbles and shrill cries. He seemed at once bored and thrilled to be there, depending on who he looked upon. Jacob scoffed when the man gave a spiritless wave towards him.

"Porridge, my dear chap," Rommond said, grasping both his hands, and holding them as if he were a lady.

"Porridge?" Jacob said to Taberah beneath his breath. *I hope that's a nickname.*

Porridge blushed and giggled as Rommond greeted him. "Oh!" he cried. "Rommond, it's been too long, my charming boy. Oh! I've got all these doodads and doohickeys, and I don't know where to put them!" He put his delicate hand over his mouth, as if he had said too much.

"I've been busy, of course," Rommond explained, as Porridge linked his arm and began walking with him around the cargo bay. Where they were going was anyone's guess. Jacob guessed in circles.

"You're a wanted man, Rommond," the merchant said, biting the knuckles of his left hand as if he could not bear to say it, "by more than just the Regime."

"Don't remind me," the general grumbled.

"I've got to remind you, my dear dandy of a friend, or I could lose one of my best customers!"

"You won't be losing me," Rommond said.

Porridge took off his purple polka-dot hat, as if he had already lost him. The merchant's golden-brown curls danced upon his crown as he shook his head at the notion.

"Oh, Rommond, dear boy," Porridge said, seeming quite concerned. "The Treasury offered money for any information on your whereabouts."

"I hope you said nothing."

"You know me, pickle. I'm a loyal merchant to a loyal customer, and you're as loyal as they get. That said, I suppose it was really the Treasury that was paying me most of those times." He giggled uncontrollably.

"Without me," Rommond said grimly, "without the Resistance, they wouldn't be paying you at all."

"And without the Regime, there'd be no Resistance. Shall we thank the Iron Emperor then?"

Rommond grumbled.

"You seem a little more vengeful than usual," the merchant noted.

"I don't sleep well these days," Rommond said.

"I haven't seen you like this since ... well, you know."

Rommond paused to take a deep breath. "I had to leave Dustdelving behind."

"So I heard."

"Then you already know why I'm more vengeful than usual. If your home had been taken, you would be too."

"Haven't got a home, plum," the merchant said. "Saves me the trouble of losing it."

"Let's be thankful, then, that the Regime's submersibles don't reach too deep."

"Let's be hopeful," Porridge said, as if he was not quite as confident on the matter. "Tell me, General, when are you going to launch this 'perfect assault' of yours?"

"What do you mean?"

"Well, you've been saving up all the gizmos and gadgets. When's, what is it you call it, H-Hour?"

"Someone forced my hand," Rommond said, glancing at Taberah. "Everything's in motion now."

"Ah then," the merchant said, "that explains the urgent trade. Let me guess ... the final piece in the puzzle?"

"Not the final piece, but it's an important one."

Jacob expected to see something sinister. A

detonator. A reactor. Something that could go boom. The crew hauled a pile of wooden panes into the room.

"What is it?" Jacob asked.

"Can't you guess?" the merchant replied, as if offended.

"Guessing's never been my game."

They unfolded the pieces. "It's a sail, peach," the merchant said.

Jacob looked at Rommond. "So your next toy is a ship?" He had enough water for a lifetime by now. At least it would no longer be above him.

Rommond smiled like a child. "A ship of the skies," he said.

Jacob sighed. So the water would be far below him then.

Porridge stayed only long enough to collect his fee, which was extortionate, and share a glass of sherry with Rommond, from a bottle the general had paid extortionate prices on before. Everyone else was ushered out of the cargo bay, and the folded-up sail was carried down to the ironworks, where the mechanics immediately began work on connecting it to the airship.

"Must dash," Porridge said. "A merchant never rests."

"That must make me a merchant then," the general replied.

Porridge placed his hand on Rommond's cheek and shook his head. "You used to be so happy."

Rommond sighed.

"You have to let him go," Porridge said. "Keeping that plaque isn't helping."

Rommond removed Porridge's hand from his face. "You could offer me any trade for it, and I would refuse. I would not trade away my time with him, nor even trade away the pain."

"Fair enough, sweetie," the merchant said. "Well, you know how to reach me. Down here I'm all ears. Oh! Aren't I clever?"

"Goodbye," Rommond said, tilting his cap slightly.

The trader left, and Rommond returned to his room, where he poured himself a second sherry. He stood before the plaque with Brooklyn's name on it. He could still see the markings where he had pulled it from the landship, when he tried to save it like he should have saved the man he loved. *Sometimes I think it's easier to keep this, than to keep my memories of you.*

The general was deep in brooding, his own kind of meditation, when he felt the submarine lurch. He knew that feeling. They were rising quickly. "Alson," he called over the intercom. "Did you just blow a ballast tank?"

There was no answer.

Then he saw a small light flicker on the wall. He stood up suddenly, glad to have some distraction, though not glad to see what kind of distraction it was.

Enemy submarines had just been spotted.

Chapter Twenty

THE ART OF SILENCE

A light in every room flashed five times, followed by a pause before they blinked the same number again. There was a chart beneath the light, which told the crew what each series of flickers meant. One was dive. Two was surface. Three was battle. Four was fire. Five was silence.

Jacob had half-heartedly read the signs before, but he still had to consult one now to see exactly what it meant. He hardly needed to, however, for the submarine's systems began to shut down, one by one, leaving only the bare essentials running. First to cease was the propeller, which produced the most noise via cavitation, and the submarine glided to a halt in the darkness, with most of its interior lights put out or dimmed to a bare minimum.

"Silent run," Rommond whispered over the intercom, like a phantom voice.

Whistler tapped gently at Jacob's door. It was such a weak knock that it would never have been heard under any under circumstances, but now it sounded loud, too loud.

"What's going on?" he whispered.

"I think we're hiding," Jacob whispered back.

"From what?" Whistler asked.

Jacob was wondering that too. He thought the Regime did not have submarines that could dive as deep as the Lifemaker. Rommond insisted the enemy's vessels were powered purely by steam, while the Resistance's monstrous underwater ship had a potent diesel engine. Jacob wondered then if the attacker was another of the marine wildlife. If that was the case, he thought, then maybe it did not need sight or sound to find them.

Jacob could hear his breathing, and Whistler's heavier pants. There was something about the silence, about not knowing, that was more unnerving than the chaos of the abyss. It could be anything out there. It could be anything inside as well.

"I don't like this," Whistler said. "Can we find Rommond?"

"Let's just sit still for a moment and see what's up."

Whistler crept over to Jacob and sat down on the bed beside him. He clutched the edge of the mattress with both hands, and he looked as though he was about to flee at any moment. Both of them glanced around the room at every creak, at every tiny ping. Each sound made Whistler flinch, but it was the silence made Jacob nervous.

"You'll be all right," Jacob whispered, putting his arm around Whistler's shoulder. He was not so sure he could say the same about himself.

The sonar beeped periodically in the command room, which was otherwise immersed in silence.

There were no valves turned, no switches clicked, and no levers pulled. Everyone stared at the sonar screen, and everyone listened anxiously for its foreboding beeps.

Ping. Each pulse had an unnerving echo. No one could quite breathe until the entire sound faded. But the long pause between each ping was just as unsettling. It was like knowing that Death was out there, and waiting for it to arrive.

Ping. Rommond looked at Taberah and then at Alson, who looked to each other also with anxious faces. The sound came a little earlier. That meant the enemy was a little closer.

Ping. The pace was quickening. The echoes had barely faded before a new one begun. *Ping.* Hearts beat in unison with the sonar, and now they were beating faster. Breaths were shallow. Pulses were quick.

Ping. Not even a second in-between. *Ping.* No chance for breath. *Ping.* They had arrived.

The sonar was muted, and Taberah put on her earphones to continue to listen to its haunting beeps. For the rest of the crew, they no long needed it. They could plainly hear the sound of the submarine above, its spinning propellers, its turning rudders.

Rommond looked up, and everyone else looked up instinctively. *They're right above us*, he thought. Several members of the crew looked to him anxiously, seeking some advice, some command. He gently pressed the index finger of his right hand against his lips. Silence was their only order. *Be silent, or be dead.*

* * *

In Jacob's room, the silence was sandwiched between the noise of their minds and the sound of the submarine above. Whistler trembled periodically, and Jacob pulled him closer to calm him down. He was glad the boy was there. There was something about looking out for someone else that helped him suppress his own fear. When Whistler shook, he knew he could not tremble in return.

"Can we go find Rommond?" Whistler whispered into his ear. He looked as eager as ever.

Jacob nodded. It was probably better to move quietly about the ship, giving them a purpose, something to keep their minds off the silence inside the submarine, and the tremendous din outside. Something to keep them from screaming out.

They crept out of the room, taking the smallest and gentlest of steps. Whistler was so light of foot he could have trudged around and made less noise than Jacob's most laboured sneak. No matter how gently he placed his feet down on the floor, it always seemed like they made a bellowing noise. At the Hope factory light may have been an enemy, and in the abyss it may have been a friend, but beneath the ocean sound betrayed everyone.

They found the head cook Karlsif wandering around the deck, making no effort at all to cushion his steps. He seemed lost, more than usual, and he clutched his hat in both hands as if it were his fleeing nerves.

"There's no one in the kitchen," he said when he saw them.

"Keep your voice down," Jacob whispered harshly.

Karlsif pointed his hat towards the direction of the kitchen. "There's no one there, but I can hear them!" His hand trembled, and his whole body followed suit. Panic emerged from the abyss of his mind, which it had conquered, and his heart, which it had corrupted.

Just as it seemed like the cook was about to scream out, Jacob seized him and held him against the wall, cupping his hand over Karlsif's mouth. He could feel the cook's moist breath against his palm as he tried to scream and shout, as he tried to let the panic out, where it could find other minds and hearts to conquer and corrupt.

Whistler pressed his own body against the cook to stop him from fleeing, though his contribution did not make much of a difference. What it did do, however, was distract him from his own fears. Karlsif had terror enough for them all.

They stayed like this for what felt like eternity, fighting against the prospect of sound, which promised them the prospect of death. Throughout the ship the crew held their breath, hoping not even to let out a tiny hiss of air that might announce their whereabouts. The submarines above continued to grind by, creating all of the sounds that some aboard the Lifemaker desperately wanted to make.

Yet Karlsif wanted more than any other to be heard. He mumbled through Jacob's hand, and Jacob tried to clench tighter, to crush the sounds between his fingers. He felt the hot breath and saliva on his hand, and Karlsif's struggling lips, but he knew that the discomfort he felt would be nothing compared to that if they were caught.

But Karlsif fought for the freedom of his tongue, and fear gave him strength. He turned his head this way and that, shifting Jacob's grip upon his face. His eyes bulged, threatening any who looked upon them, and Jacob tried not to look, but he had to see where he needed to place his hand to smother the sounds.

Yet silence is a vacuum; it begs to be filled. Karlsif bit Jacob's fingers, and in that bite there was the promise that he would make a meal out of them if he could not speak. Jacob recoiled for a second, but it was enough to trumpet out some words.

"I did it," Karlsif said, half a whisper, half a cry for help.

Jacob questioned him with his confusion.

"I blew the tank," the cook confessed. "We have to get out! I have to get back up there! I can't *breathe* down here. I'm suffocating, soldier! Don't you see? We're all suffocating in this death trap, this cooking pot. We're all going to boil in the ocean!"

Jacob muffled his ramblings once more, but it was harder than ever to fight against them. Fragments of words escaped the cage of his hand, calling out for rescue by the Regime.

The rescuers must have heard, because the sounds of the propellers and rudders suddenly stopped. A new silence emerged, announcing something different, something coming.

In the control room the tension was more palpable than ever.

"They've spotted us," Alson said. "They're turning

'round."

Rommond sighed and pulled a lever down aggressively, setting off a deafening alarm. The sound contrasted starkly with the quiet flashing lights that began their agonising moment of silence.

"All hands," Rommond called out over the intercom. "Battle stations."

Chapter Twenty-one

WAR BENEATH THE WAVES

There was a frenzy aboard the Lifemaker, with people racing to their stations, and preparing and arming the torpedoes.

"Number one armed and ready," one of the torpedo loaders called out over the intercom.

"Have we got a lock?" Rommond asked in the control room.

"We have a lock," Taberah said. "Twelve metres ahead."

"Fire one," Rommond ordered.

"Firing one," was the response, followed by a slight shudder in the ship as the torpedo left its bay and went straight for the submarine directly ahead of the Lifemaker. The missile carved a path through the water, which any sonar would have picked up, but it was too late for the other vessel to turn or move. It exploded beneath the sea, a marriage of fire and water.

"We've got another on our tail," Taberah said. "Closing fast."

"Aft torpedo team," Rommond called into his microphone. "Status?"

"Three and four, armed and rearing to go."

Taberah sent the co-ordinates of the enemy vessel over the submarine's telegraph line, allowing the crew in the aft of the ship to align the torpedo properly. "We have a lock," she said, when the signal was acknowledged as received and acted upon.

"Fire three," Rommond said.

The torpedo launched straight into the advancing Regime submarine, knocking out its engines, but it failed to destroy it.

"Shall we fire four?"

"No," Rommond said. "Save it for the next one."

But there was little time to save anything, for the Regime sent submarines by the dozen, and though they were tiny compared to the Lifemaker, they were so numerous that they were almost certain to overwhelm the larger ship.

"We've got locks on bow and stern," Taberah said.

"Fire two and four," Rommond said, "and get those bays loaded again quickly."

But the swarm kept coming, and it kept growing. Even as the Lifemaker depleted its supply of torpedoes, and submarine after submarine exploded beneath the waves, the Regime continued to replenish its forces. They came from all angles, like a pack of vultures for a wounded prey.

"God, Rommond, they're everywhere!" Taberah cried. "We've got some on port and starboard."

The sides of the submarine were particularly vulnerable, because the torpedoes only fired from the front and back. Several vessels on either side opened fire, aiming much smaller torpedoes at the Lifemaker. Most of these simply bounced off the hull, for it was reinforced to withstand a battering, and a few of them missed entirely.

"They can't get through!" Taberah cheered.

"Don't get too hopeful yet," Rommond cautioned. "The sting of the bee is worst in a swarm."

The Regime continued its unending onslaught. That was how they came into power. Sheer numbers. And as the human population dwindled, the demon ranks grew and grew. Those born in Altadas were still young—mere children—but they would soon replenish the fallen who assailed the Lifemaker as if not a single one among them mattered, bar the illustrious Iron Emperor.

"There's too many," Alson said. "I can't navigate through them. They're like mines!"

"We could ram them," Taberah suggested. "The hull can take the stress, right?"

Rommond paused for a moment while he contemplated the idea, but he did not have long to think. The victors in war were often those who made the quick decisions. He knew well, however, that some of the losers in war lost because they did not think things through.

"Go ahead," he said. "Knock them out of the way."

Alson advanced the Lifemaker at medium speed, grazing off many of the smaller vessels, and pushing several of them away. They crashed into one another, and a few of them tried to turn, and a few barely managed to get out of the way in time.

But still they came.

"Fire all noisemakers," Rommond ordered. The noisemakers were small devices that mimicked the sounds of the Lifemaker, helping draw enemy attention, and enemy fire. Though to all appearances they were nothing like the vessel they launched from, in the sound-dominated world beneath the sea, they showed up on the Regime's sonar as dozens of doppelgangers, confounding their captains, and confusing their torpedoes.

Alson launched the noisemakers, which caused a flurry of fire outside. Submarines turned to face their new phantom foes, and torpedoes were wasted like bullets on ghosts. The Lifemaker advanced through the horde, leaving behind many of them in the frenzy, but not all were fooled by the decoys. They might have made all the right sounds, but the Lifemaker made the same ones too.

"Drop mines," Rommond commanded.

The hatches opened on small tubes at the back of the Lifemaker, from which fell dozens of small floating mines. These were much smaller than the ones the Regime used, and while this made them easier to navigate, it also made them harder to detect. Many submarines that pursued the Lifemaker exploded as they came into contact with the mines, and this might have caused some hesitation in the other captains, were it not for the fact that the Iron Emperor would not permit such a thing. As their comrades died around them, the Regime soldiers pushed on for the death of their enemies, or for the glory of their own demise.

The Lifemaker thundered through the waters at its fastest speeds, knocking aside reinforcements that seemed to emerge from all directions. In time the entire supply of torpedoes was depleted, the noisemakers had ceased making noise, and the mines were left behind with the debris and bodies of the dozens of submarines they claimed.

And still they came.

The Lifemaker darted through the ocean, but the other submarines were just as fast. They swarmed around the ship, matching its speed, as if the vessel was their hive. They gathered in close, until their hulls touched the hull of the greater ship, and no weapon could disperse them, and no tactic could evade them.

"They're breaking in!" Alson called.

Taberah looked at Rommond, and though the glance was grim, she looked as determined as ever. She left the room to confront the enemy. If they could not win at sea, she would win on land.

Metal clamps gripped the sides of the submarine, glass tubes formed airtight passages from the attacking submarines to the Lifemaker, and steel drills bored holes into the hull, giving free passage inside. Entrances appeared here and there across the ship, and even when Regime soldiers at one of these were repelled, they flooded into the vessel from another location, bringing the battle of the sea inside the ship.

Chapter Twenty-two

BOARDING PARTY

Though the Regime's submarines were much smaller than the Lifemaker, they were teeming with soldiers, many of whom now boarded the Lifemaker, fighting their way through, firing at anyone and everyone in sight.

Some of the Resistance soldiers were caught off guard, and were gunned down at their stations, and some were shot while racing to their posts. Others were more prepared, barricading themselves in rooms, or building makeshift fortifications for cover, or charging the advancing enemy, or firing fanatically into the openings that appeared.

Jacob and Whistler bumped into Taberah as she charged down the corridor, her hair a fiery halo, as if the hordes of Hell were behind her. Jacob knew well, however, that she was not running from the demons; she was running towards them. He grabbed her by the arm and pulled her into a nearby room. Whistler ran in after them.

"Where are you going?" Jacob asked.

"To fight!" she growled, as if she might fight him too.

"You haven't got a weapon."

"I've got my fists."

"You're not the Copper Matron."

"You're a good few muscles short of her yourself."

"It's too dangerous out there," Jacob said. "Are you trying to get yourself killed?"

"I'm heading to the armoury."

The armoury that Jacob remembered visiting previously was some distance away, a route that would likely bring them under enemy fire.

"That's not exactly close by," he said.

"We can't just sit here and do nothing!" Taberah roared.

Jacob shook his head. "We'll need to be quick," he said. "And careful." He knew the latter was not a word Taberah used often in her diaries.

"Can we not just seal up this room?" Whistler asked. He was already shaking from the sounds outside.

Taberah gave her answer by charging out the door, shouting as she went.

"I guess not," Jacob said, edging out behind her. Whistler followed quickly, and Jacob shielded him as best he could. In many ways, however, Taberah shielded them all, for she raced down the corridor and jumped on one of the Regime soldiers who was passing through. He yelped as she dug her nails into his face, and he clambered and struggled, and pushed back with her against the wall, casting her from him. As soon as she fell, she caught the man by the knees and pulled him to the ground. He collapsed and struck his head against the steel floor, turning it red.

Jacob and Whistler caught up with her.

Taberah rummaged through the body. "He doesn't have a weapon."

"Cutbacks," Jacob said. "They affect us all."

She rolled her eyes at him and continued to search the soldier. Jacob joined her, and Whistler crouched down beside them, but refused to touch the body. Taberah uncovered a series of drawings and design documents of the Lifemaker.

"It seems they know more about us than we thought," Jacob said.

"Rommond will be furious," Taberah replied.

"Is he not already?"

"I don't think you've really seen him angry yet."

They searched more, finding an ID badge, which showed that the man she had killed was not, in fact, a soldier, but a surveyor, likely one of several brought to find weaknesses in the Lifemaker that the Regime could exploit.

"He wasn't going to kill us then," Whistler said despondently.

"It doesn't matter," Taberah said. "He was in the way, and he would have called for backup."

They stood up, and Taberah rubbed her back.

"You know, I don't think you should be throwing yourself at people while pregnant," Jacob said.

Taberah glared at him, as if he might be next. "Then get me a gun."

Rommond was already out in force, clearing the top deck and sealing Alson in the control room. He gave her one command: if it all came to the worst, sink the ship.

Boulder and Alakovi were given similar commands through the onboard telegraph system. They were told to seal off the lower levels, and, if necessary, to scuttle the submarine and sink all of the Resistance vehicles and weapons, rather than let the Regime acquire them.

For his part, it was typical Rommond. He announced over the intercom the parts of the ship he was heading to, to "liberate," only to appear elsewhere, guns blazing. Then he would show up correctly at places he announced, but the Regime troops there expected it to be another bluff. The result was chaos in the Regime ranks, for no one truly knew where Rommond and his men would appear, if they even showed up at all.

Not only did Rommond use these feints and bluffs; he made full use of the ventilation shafts, and other obscure routes and passages, to come out on top of troops aiming their weapons down the main corridors.

These tactics worked wonders against all of the Regime soldiers, bar one: Domas. The enemy general stepped onto the submarine from his own, and the ranks immediately fell into place, and they had a second general to fear.

Taberah led the way to the armoury, half-running, half-crouching, and stopping here and there to catch her breath or nurse a cramp. Jacob tried on several occasions to get ahead of her, but she bit through her pain and pushed forward, passing him by, insistent that she knew the way better than he. She did, but he was not concerned about the route; he was concerned about her.

They met no resistance for the first fifteen minutes, turning corners without the aid of mirrors, storming passages without the help of grenades. How Jacob wished to have Soasa there; he did not mind if she barred his way, so long as she barred the way of the enemy too.

Then they heard harsh footsteps ahead, and by the sound of it, there were many soldiers passing through. They turned back, Taberah somewhat reluctantly, and crept along the way they had come, until they met a stairwell up to a higher deck.

"Let's go up," Jacob whispered.

"There's no armoury on that deck," Taberah said. "We need weapons."

"We need to get out of the way," Jacob insisted. He took a few steps up, pulling Whistler with him. Taberah glanced back at the corridor and listened to the fading footsteps.

"Come on," Jacob said.

"Wait," she replied. "I think I can make it now."

He tried to stop her, but she ran back to where they had just been, and the footsteps grew louder again.

Rommond had cleared the entire top deck of Regime soldiers, and was picking off groups of enemy combatants on the other floors. He sent his lieutenants on similar missions, while the other troops were ordered to shore up and defend the newly-secured decks.

Rommond was concerned, however, that the Regime would opt to bypass the control room altogether and aim for the ironworks below, where his valuable cache of vehicles was stored. That Boulder and Alakovi, his best engineers, might fall with them also played on his mind. He knew that the Resistance could not win if it lost its technological edge.

He made for the lower deck, creeping through the ventilation shafts, careful not to cause too much noise. His knees were already aching. He was not a young man any more. But his hands were still strong, and his gun was still loaded.

He came out on the deck above the forbidden floor, the entrance to which he noticed had been nailed shut. He went into a nearby quarters and pulled out a small rug, which was barely big enough to cover the hatch. It was probably a foolish ploy, but it was better than nothing.

"Well, well, well," a voice said from the corridor behind Rommond. He knew immediately who it was, and turned slowly to find Domas standing there.

Rommond did not dally. He fired a shot as soon as he caught a glimpse of the general. Had it been any other soldier, they would have fallen to his gunfire, but Domas was fast, and he slipped around the corner with a demonic speed.

"Not quite the welcome I was looking for," Domas shouted.

"My gun is even more welcoming than that," Rommond said. "Come out to greet it."

"I would have preferred to have a look at you again," Domas said, "without that long-haired brat you hauled along with you. And I don't mean Taberah, though she fits the bill as well."

"I'm not one of your machine men, Domas," Rommond replied. "You can't push my buttons so easily."

"Really, Rommond?" Domas called out. "Then why have you been hiding away? Was Brooklyn so much to you that you couldn't function without him?"

Rommond let out a slow sigh, trying not to let Domas hear it. "Last I checked, I just fired a bullet your way."

"Last *I* checked," Domas said with glee, "you missed."

Rommond moved slightly to his left, where he could see part of the corridor that intersected with his own. He fired a bullet at the far wall, which ricocheted into the other corridor where Domas was hiding.

"Woah, now!" Domas said. "That was a close one. You'd swear I pushed a button for that."

"I've got six bullets left, Domas," Rommond said. "Keep pushing."

He fired another shot, letting the wall help him. It was the wall of the Lifemaker. *His* ship, his submarine. He knew that it would help. He could not see Domas, but the walls could see everything. He heard Domas shuffling out of the way as the bullet bounced off the metal.

"You don't believe in playing fair, now, do you, Rommond?" Domas asked. Rommond did not reply. He was aiming another shot.

"Good," Domas said, "because I don't either."

Suddenly a cannister rolled down the corridor, spewing smoke and gas as it went. Rommond quickly grabbed his gas mask from his belt and placed it over his mouth. He did not duck or dodge, but instead stopped the cannister with his boot and kicked it back.

"We can play games like this all night," Rommond said. "Or you can face me like a man."

Domas cackled, as if it were laughing gas. "According to you, I'm not a man."

"Even if you were human, Domas, you would be far from a man. Come out, coward, and face me."

"Not while you still have five bullets left."

Rommond fired again. The ping was reassuring at first, but then it showed that it was just hitting more metal, not flesh. Had Rommond been facing one of Domas' machine men, that would have been a good thing.

"There," Rommond called. "There aren't five left."

Domas laughed. "I used to love this, Rommond, back when we moved trenches inches forward and backwards. The banter made it all worthwhile."

"I preferred the bullets," Rommond said, firing another. He heard Domas gasp as he flung himself out of the bullet's rebound. Rommond cursed in his mind and pursed his lips, to avoid cursing out loud and giving Domas any satisfaction.

"Four more tries," Domas said. "It's a bit like blind man's bluff, isn't it?"

"Except I'm not bluffing." Another shot. Another miss.

"Are you sure?" Domas shouted out to him. The

echo made it harder to pinpoint him. "It doesn't look like you're really trying."

Rommond fired two rounds, aimed slightly apart, hoping Domas would dodge the first, only to enter the path of the second. He heard Domas shuffling back and forth, cackling as he went.

"Good old Ricochet Rommond! Good try, Rommond, good try! You know, in the Iron Empire we don't award people who try. Is the Resistance different? Did you earn your pips from trying?"

One more try, Rommond thought. He took a deep breath, and could almost hear Domas taking one of his own. Sounds became magnified in that moment. He heard the click of the trigger, the rotation of the barrel, and the ping of the bullet. He heard the feet of Domas, the shuffle, the shimmy. Then he heard Domas' laugh, which betrayed no sign of injury.

"Another try, another pip," Domas said. "Why, you should be in for a promotion." He edged out into the corridor with a broad smile and a raised gun, with not a single bullet spent. Rommond kept his own pistol pointed at the demon.

"I can count, Rommond," Domas said. "Your six bullets are used up."

Rommond smiled, and fired his seventh.

Three soldiers descended on Taberah, and Jacob descended on the troops, knocking one out cold with a steel pipe, which another soldier knocked from his hand just as easily.

"Run!" he cried to Taberah, and she ran before he even finished the word.

One of the remaining soldiers began to make for her, but Jacob grabbed him and pulled him back. The soldier reached for his gun, but Jacob knocked it from his hand. The soldier struggled to reach down for it, and Jacob struggled to prevent him from doing so. The second soldier punched Jacob, knocking him down, and he would have kept punching were it not for Whistler pelting him with nuts and bolts from the nearby debris. The soldier turned to the boy, seething anger, and dripping blood from the small cuts on his forehead. He charged after Whistler as the boy ran back up the stairs.

Jacob continued his battle. They pushed each other back and forth against the metal walls, sending steel echoes down the corridor, chased by the echoes of their heaves and pants, and shouts and grunts. The soldier hauled Jacob away from the wall and tripped him, but Jacob clung to the man's uniform, pulling him down with him. They rolled along the ground, punching and kicking, bashing and clawing, and reaching out for anything that might stop the flaying of the other.

Jacob seized the iron bar and swung it down. The soldier stopped fighting, and stopped breathing. Jacob grabbed the gun from the ground and stood up, panting harshly.

He paused for a moment and looked to his right, to the path Taberah had taken. Then he looked to his left, where Whistler had fled, and where the other soldier had chased him. If only he could take them both, using the iron bar in one and the gun in the other. But he had to make a choice.

He turned left and ran up the stairs to the higher level, and prayed to all gods that Whistler was still fleeing. Jacob hoped he had not taken too long to make his choice.

Taberah continued, unhindered, towards the armoury. At any other time, she would have praised the length of the submarine, a testament to Brooklyn's epic designs. Now she cursed it, but she did not curse his memory.

She was much closer now, and she fought the urge to race ahead, which was a powerful urge inside her. Something seemed to slow her down. She did not know why she hesitated. Then she stopped when she thought she heard voices. She strained her hearing, but could not make them out, or what they said. She wondered if it was Jacob or Whistler, calling her back—or doom calling her forward.

She crept closer to the origin of those sounds, and listened closely. She heard a familiar voice.

"Good old Ricochet Rommond!" it said. *Domas*.

Stronger than the urge to race ahead, and the compulsion to find the owners of the voices, was the desire to kill. She made for the passages from where the sounds emanated, down those long hallways, and though she had condemned those very walkways, when she thought of Domas, she used every curse.

The bullet struck Domas in the stomach, and he cried out and grasped at the wound, where the blood leaked out like any human. He dropped his pistol, stumbled to the side and reached out for the wall to support himself.

"You!" he shouted, wagging a bloody finger at Rommond. "Always with your ploys."

"I thought that's what you liked about me," Rommond replied, wishing the ploy involved another bullet.

"It's fun to play the games," Domas coughed, "not to lose."

"Don't play then if you cannot bear to lose."

"Did you tell that to Brooklyn, Rommond? Or did you gamble him as well?"

Rommond grasped the handle of his gun tightly, digging his fingers into the reassuring leather grip. He tried not to let Domas' words dig into his heart.

"It seems I only need to keep pressing that same button," Domas said, spitting out some blood, as if spitting on Brooklyn's grave.

"Go ahead," Rommond said, taking a step forward. He had counted the number of steps he would need to reach Domas, who was still very close to the intersection, and very close to his fallen gun. Eight steps. If Rommond was quick, he could end this. If he was not, he could end himself.

"Can you reach me," Domas mused, "before I reach my gun? I see you working it out, Rommond. I wonder if you used to mouth words when reading as a child. Me? I read people like you."

Rommond took another step forward. Slow and steady. Domas was a bigger and stronger man, who cast a big and daunting shadow. Rommond knew that he could not win a wrestle, even if Domas was badly wounded. They had played that game before, and

Rommond lost. Brute force was not his way.

"So, what will it be, Rommond?" Domas asked. "A knife to the gut? You'll have to reach for your boot to get that. By then I can reach for mine. Or my gun. You're not a spring chicken any more. Can you make it?"

Rommond took another step, just as Domas leaned a little closer to the ground, arm outstretched.

"I'm not a prophet," Rommond said, "but someone dies tonight."

Domas showed his teeth; it might have been a smile, were it not for his obvious pain. "Did you read that in my blood, soothsayer?"

Another step on one side, another reach on the other. Somewhere they would meet in the middle—in the no-man's land, where no demon could stay either.

Then Rommond thought he heard someone approaching. He looked over Domas' shoulder and saw Taberah there, panting and clenching her fists. How many steps she needed to reach Domas, he could not tell.

"So," Domas said, dwelling on the word, elongating it as if it were the measure of his life. He caught a glimpse of Taberah from the corner of his eye, and he reached a little closer to the gun. "It seems we have a late entry to the game."

Taberah made the first move. She raced forward, and Rommond ran, and Domas reached. The three of them met in the middle, where already blood was spilt.

Domas seized his gun, and pointed quick, and fired quicker, stopping Rommond in his tracks.

Taberah leapt at Domas, but he turned to her and grabbed her tight. In a moment, he pulled her back around the corner of the intersection and kicked open a door that led to the other half of the ship. Rommond was winded and wounded, yet he followed quickly—but not quickly enough. As he reached the door Domas had hauled Taberah through, it slammed in his face. He heard the rotation of the wheel that sealed it shut, and saw through the small window that Domas was pulling Taberah away into the darkness.

Chapter Twenty-three

THE FINAL WHISTLE

What Whistler lacked in strength, he made up for in speed. It was one of the few things he was certain of about himself, but as he ran from the Regime soldier, and prepared to run from the soldier's bullets, he felt that certainty crumble away.

He managed to get up to the next level and through one of the long corridors before the soldier made it up, but he was jarred by the heavy footfalls, and he thought that speed might not be enough if his pursuer had longer strides.

Whistler ducked into a metal tube before the soldier could see him, and he crawled quickly through it, cringing as his hands and knees clattered off the metal casing. He heard the footsteps drawing closer, so he halted and held his breath.

The soldier passed by, stamping upon the ground as he went. His shadow seemed to linger behind, as if it had spotted Whistler's hideout. From the corner of his eye, the boy thought it was reaching out to grab him.

Please find me, Rommond, he pleaded. He knew that if anyone could defeat this soldier, it was him. As the seconds ticked by, and seemed like minutes, and felt like hours, he started to pray for anyone to come by, anyone with a weapon, anyone with a gun.

In time it seemed that his prayers were answered. He heard shouts and gunfire, and he could tell that Resistance soldiers had happened upon the scene, but when he glanced out he saw them dead upon the ground, and the Regime soldier was still standing, his gun smoking.

"You need to learn respect, boy!" the soldier shouted. He lashed a metal ball-bearing across the chamber, just as Whistler had struck him with a bolt. It rattled off the metal pylons, but it rattled Whistler more.

"Learn it from my gun," the soldier boomed, before unloading a round throughout the chamber. The Iron Emperor himself could have been marching through those halls and it would not have mattered, so long as the soldier struck down the boy who dared draw blood from him.

The gunfire was mimicked by Whistler's chattering teeth. He hugged his arms and tried to hold his breath, but it escaped from him every now and then as a bullet flew by dangerously close.

He hid in the darkness, but it seemed from the corner of his eye that his own shadow stood out, as if betraying him. He felt a sudden urge to flee, to find a better hiding spot, but the problem with fleeing on the Lifemaker was that there was nowhere really to run to, and the problem with hiding was that the Regime was searching every hiding place.

"I know you're hiding," the soldier said. "Not so brave now, huh?" He tapped his gun on every tube, on every box, on every pillar and piston, on anything in sight. The sound was even more frightening than the bullets, because it sounded like he was drawing closer again.

Whistler peeped out from the tube and saw that the soldier was looking in every crevice as he passed. It was only a matter of moments before he would look where the boy now hid. Whistler knew he had to get out of there, had to run. He was fast, but he knew he could not outrun bullets. He had to find a way off that floor, find a way back to where the Resistance was still fighting—if anyone else was still alive.

From that vantage point he could see a pile of metal barrels across the room, in the furthest corner from where the soldier now searched. Behind these a half-ladder clung to the wall, leading up to a rampart that led to the next deck. If he could just get to it in time, and survive the run, he might be saved. Yet it seemed awfully far away.

The soldier knocked over a large storage box, emptying its contents to the floor in a thunderous spray. This was Whistler's opportunity. He leapt out from the metal tube and raced across the room. He knew the soldier saw him, and he heard the angry rattle of gunfire in his wake. He threw himself on top of the barrels and grabbed hold of the ladder. He was almost at the top when he felt the soldier grab his ankle and pull him down. He slipped a rung and cried out, and he tried to kick, but the soldier's massive fist engulfed his leg, and he was dragged to the ground. He yelped as he fell, and grunted as his head hit the ground, and when he tried to get up he was stopped by the butt of the soldier's gun.

"The cat always gets the mouse," the soldier said. But cats did not have guns.

"On your knees," the soldier ordered. That day he was also an executioner.

Whistler held himself up on his elbows. How he wished he could make some brazen remark like Jacob might. How he wished he could stare down the barrel of a gun, and stare down Death. How he wished he could defy the soldier, or defy his own trembling limbs. But he could not. The soldier hauled him to his feet, then tapped the back of his knees with the gun until he knelt down to await his fate.

He felt the icy touch of the gun's barrel, and he was frozen. He clenched his eyes shut, as if that would somehow save him from his doom. If he could not see it, it did not exist. How he wished for fairy tales, for happy endings, and how he hated that he knew that horror stories were more real. It was part of growing up, and he wanted that so bad. And now he feared he would never get to.

And yet he hoped. He did not want it all to end, that he might no longer feel pain; he wanted to live so he could still feel those brief moments of pleasure, those fleeting times of happiness. Now, as he knew it all would end, he wanted it to continue all the more.

The gun marked a large O on his forehead, where it would mark his end. He tried to be brave, to take it like a man, to *die* like a man. But all he could do was tremble like a child. He did not realise for several seconds that tears were pouring down his face, as if to flee the site of the carnage to come.

How the soldier must have loved that Whistler shook before him. The more the boy knelt down and cowered to the ground, the more the soldier must have felt taller and more powerful. Whistler knew all this deep inside. He knew it was why the soldier delayed the kill. It was not about the end itself; it was about making the prey understand that the end was coming, that the when was in the predator's hands. As much as the predator controlled the gun, he controlled the prey. It was a kind of primal power. It was its own kind of drug.

"This is what you get," the soldier said, circling the tip of the gun across Whistler's forehead, ensuring that he could always feel it, "when you mess with the Regime."

Whistler wanted it to end, one way or another. The waiting was torture.

"I kill dozens every day," the soldier said. "Most of them get a quick death. You could have had that, but instead you had to try and fight."

He moved the gun down the ridge of Whistler's nose. "I could start here," he said, before moving the gun to the boy's right cheek, which was still bandaged from the burns. "It looks like someone's already started here. Or maybe it's better beneath the chin." He moved the gun to Whistler's neck and nudged up his chin. "No," he said, moving the gun back to the boy's forehead. "It's better between the eyes. That way you can almost see the bullet coming."

This was it. Whistler clenched his teeth, and clenched his fists, and raised his shoulders. He waited for the bang, for the blackness, for the pain, and then the painlessness. The wait might have only been seconds, but if those seconds were to be all he had left to live, his mind instinctively tried to make them last. He waited for the end of his brief life, and whatever awaited him thereafter.

Then he heard a whack, and the soldier grunted and collapsed.

"No," he heard, and he opened his eyes to see Jacob standing there clutching a metal bar. "It's better on the back of the head, where you can't see it coming at all."

Jacob helped Whistler to his feet, and Whistler tried to straighten up and stop his trembles, to pretend as if he could have taken the soldier any minute.

"It's okay to be afraid, kid," Jacob said. "In this world, there are a lot of things to fear."

Whistler gulped and snuffled, and then looked up to Jacob. "Like you?"

Jacob smiled. "Like me."

Chapter Twenty-four

DEATHMAKER

Taberah and Domas struggled in the darkness. She kicked and fought, and he tried to hold her down and contain her flailing limbs. He used the thick muscles of his arms, but she used everything she had: her knees, her elbows, her teeth, and her nails. She scraped and scratched, bit and bashed, and when she found the bullet hole in Domas' torso, she pressed her fingers into the wound until he yelped and squealed, and then she prodded and twisted until he let her go.

She scrambled away. She knew she could not fight him like this. Teeth and nails could not defend against bullets. She decided against racing towards the door they had come in by. He had locked it tight, and it would take too long to open. It would take less time to fire the gun. She ran down the corridor, which led to several other rooms. She tried the doors on some as she passed, but most would not budge, and those few that did led into dead ends. She did not mind a dead end, so long as it was an armoury. She wished she had not been drawn by Domas' voice, wished she had found the gun supply before seeking him out. She could not help but hear Rommond berating her in her mind. Rommond was all about planning; she was all about doing, but she could not do anything here without a plan.

She continued down the corridor, turning left at the next intersection. She knew the submarine well, but she felt disorientated. The problem with the passages is that they, for the most part, all looked the same. The flickering oil lamps did not help, nor did the darkness in the places where the flames had died out. She entered one of those dark corridors now, and she did not take a lamp to guide her. It was safer in the darkness.

She heard Domas stirring far behind her. His moans echoed down the passages. It was clear that Rommond got him good. A bullet in the gut was the least he deserved. She was glad Rommond did not shoot him in the heart. She wanted that pleasure herself.

She followed the winding walkways, doubting her memory, trusting her intuition. She knew the armoury was around here somewhere. She just hoped they had not locked the doors. She looked for vents as she went, but she could not see any. The darkness plotted against all eyes.

Domas found it a struggle to get to his feet. Every muscle seemed to be connected with his stomach like a conspiracy. He cringed and groaned, and he clenched his teeth as if he could bite away the pain. He got his back against a wall and pushed himself up against it, while clutching his gut—and clutching his gun.

I hope you like your bullet more than mine, Rommond. He stumbled towards the door he had locked, and looked through the circular window, hoping to see Rommond's body slumped down upon the floor. He sighed when he saw just a few specks of blood. There was much more on this side of the door. *Let's make it two for one, then. Taberah needs to join us.*

He hobbled down the corridor Taberah had ran down. He liked a chase. Sometimes he let them run just so he could run after them, often just so he could shoot them in the back. How they fell. The faster they ran, the swifter they fell. There was pleasure in the hunt. With Taberah, the pleasure would be more.

"You know me, Taberah," Domas shouted. "Or should I call you Tabs? Did Rommond ever get as close as I did?" He scoffed and laughed, and then cringed from the pain.

He continued down the corridor, the wall supporting his body, the hunt supporting his will. He patted his hand on the emblem of the Regime on his left shoulder. A single pat for a single leader. How the Iron Emperor would commend him if he brought back Taberah's head. How he would elevate him if he heard that Rommond had fallen. But those pleasures, great as though they would be, would pale in comparison to the acts themselves. It was not about the end; it was about the means.

"Come out, Taberah," he called, banging his gun on one of the sealed doors. "You never used to hide. Isn't that a coward's game? Did you learn it from Rommond?"

He thought that would have done it. She always had more pride than sense.

"You know, I was gentle with you, Taberah," he said. "When you got hit in the Hope factory, I didn't dig my fingers into the wound. That's not very nice, now, is it? Tell me, who's the real demon?"

If he had been hunting Jacob, he knew the smuggler would have answered back. With Taberah, he did not expect a verbal reply; he expected her to come out to fight him. It was only a matter of time, a matter of enough questions asked. He kept asking.

"I've heard tell that some in the Resistance wonder about us, about our nature, what we're really like, what we really are. You can paint us with horns to justify your war against us, but we know what we are, and we know that you're not as angelic as you make out. But let me tell you something about us. We dream, just like you. And do you know who I often dream about?"

He continued down the corridor, leaning against the wall, leaving a trail of blood behind him. He had to kill Taberah before it ran out.

"Time's up," he said. "The answer, of course, is you! I remember that first year in Altadas as if it were yesterday. I always preferred my old world, but I've got to admit, the women here are a much finer specimen."

Domas heard a faint whimpering from a nearby cupboard. *That isn't like her*, he thought. *She never let me hear her cry.* He opened the cupboard door to find another woman there, cradling her bulging belly.

"Who's this?" he asked.

"M-m-marya," she said, but it was a struggle.

"Don't cower," Domas said. "Do you want the baby to come out a coward too?"

She shook her head, sending the tears in all directions.

"Oh, you don't want the baby to come out at all?" he asked, and fired his gun.

He took a moment to savour the sight. He recognised a Pure when he saw one. They had a certain glow about them, like a halo. But they were no angels. They were the ones that Chance created, the ones that somehow escaped the Birth-masters' webs. No matter how many worlds they went through, there was always a flaw; someone always escaped with the birth channels intact.

"I just killed one of your Pure," Domas shouted down the corridor, chasing Taberah with echoes. "So much for the Lifemaker. You just rounded them up for us, making it easier for the cull."

He began to tap his gun on the wall as he went, forming a rhythm like a heartbeat, a tempo to replace the heartbeats he had just ended.

"Do you know what we did in our old world?" Domas continued. "There used to be a people there, greater than your own. It took time, over a century, in fact, but we got there in the end. We wiped them all out. With you—what is it, humans?—we'll likely get there in half the time."

Still no sound or squeak. Her silence bothered him. He knew that was why she did it, why she refused to speak, refused to squeal. She got to him in a way that no one else ever had. But he knew that deep beneath the silence, she was screaming.

Taberah found the armoury after what felt like hours. She heard many of Domas' taunts. It was hard not to turn back and charge at him. She would get there, she told herself, once she found a weapon to charge with.

The armoury was mostly empty, bar the bodies. It had been raided by both Resistance and Regime soldiers, leaving very few weapons left. The few guns she found had no bullets. She threw them to the ground in anger, as if the ground were Domas. She rummaged through the mess in the room, well aware that she was making far too much noise, and almost not caring. She did not want to run forever. She wanted to fight and win, or fight and die.

She found a knife amidst the clutter, but as she took it up, the blade fell from the handle. She almost cursed aloud. It seemed that she herself was cursed. Maybe it was the Lifemaker. It had not lived up to Rommond's promise, despite all his plots and plans. Now it might become the Deathmaker for them all.

Everything she found was useless. There were no projectiles and no ammunition. There was very little that was sharp, and those that were, were not sharp enough. Even the blunt weapons, the wooden bats, were splintered and broken, as if they had already been used in the fight for control of the armoury. By the looks of it, she was not sure anyone had won.

Domas trudged forward. His determination could not stop the flow of blood, but it pushed him on.

"Some wonder why I follow the Iron Emperor,"

he mused aloud. "Some think that it is weakness to follow, but not if you follow strength. I have lived through so many wars, but they pale in comparison to the conquests he has made. Our people live and thrive because of him, because of his glorious leadership, his divine wisdom, his endless love for our people. He offers purity in a universe of impurity, where world after world mock the intended order of things."

He tapped his hand against the Regime emblem again, and bowed his head, just as he had bowed it so many times before the Iron Emperor. That was the salute, right hand upon left shoulder, head bowed, knees bent. It was humbling, but when a million soldiers made it together in unison, it was strengthening—it was empowering.

"Who do you follow, Taberah?" he asked. "You used to follow Rommond, but we all know how that went. You did a better job of stabbing him in the back than Teller tried to. So, who do you follow now? No one? Your dreams? Your ideals? No, I think you just follow yourself, and you want everyone else to follow suit, to bow down to you and call you the Iron Empress."

He laughed. He could not hear her response, but he was certain he was pushing buttons. Everyone crumbled with enough persistence. It was just a matter of finding the right combination. He knew he was close. He knew that the next line would likely break her.

"And what about your son?" he said. He waited a moment to let the words reach her ears. He did not rush his taunts. It was better to let her insecurities form their own. "Well?" he asked in time. "Don't pretend he isn't yours. We all see the resemblance. But does he follow you? You might think he does, but isn't he supposed to 'blow the whistle' on us 'demons'? Isn't that his job, his duty? How many people has he let through the net? Ardra, Daniel, Teller. Are you sure he doesn't follow us instead?"

He heard a rush of footsteps, and he smiled. He almost heard the button push. Soon he would hear the gun click.

Taberah charged at him in the darkness, screaming and brandishing a spear made from the bits and pieces she had found in the armoury. He fired the gun, but instead of falling back, she ran into the bullet, and ran into him, impaling him with the spear. He grunted and clutched his chest, and then he collapsed upon the ground.

Taberah leaned on the handle of the spear, partly to drive it deeper, party to support her. She felt the sudden pain of the gunshot wound in her abdomen, and of the energy it drained from her. Domas shouted when she twisted the spear, and then he moaned and laughed, until she twisted it again.

"How does it feel?" she asked. "*How does it feel?*"

He smiled at her, with his mouth and his eyes. She got him deep, but he got her deeper. It was like he was in her mind. Perhaps there he could not die.

She pulled out the spear, but it fell apart in her hands before she could thrust it a second time and finally end the beast before her. He laughed as she stumbled and fell, but his own pain silenced him and prevented him from standing up.

"Is this how it ends?" he asked. He could barely see her from the floor. She was slumped against a wall. "Do we both die together? What a fitting end!"

"We didn't live together," she said. "If dying together is a fitting end, we would have had to share life together."

"Didn't we?" he asked.

She said no more.

It was hours before anyone found them. The attack by the Regime was repelled, but not without substantial losses on the Resistance's side. Rommond rounded up the surviving Regime soldiers for interrogation. When he was called to where Domas and Taberah lay, he rushed to the location, and he told Jacob to keep Whistler back, for he feared the worst.

Taberah was injured, but she was still alive. So was Domas. If left untended, they both would have perished. How Rommond wanted to let Domas rot, and yet wanted to finish him once and for all.

"A sorry sight," Rommond said to the enemy general.

Domas scoffed and smiled. "Don't tell me you feel sorry for me. I know you don't."

Rommond helped Taberah up. She had spent much of her strength.

"You're wounded," Rommond said.

"So are you."

"I took the bullet out."

"I left mine in," Taberah said through gritted teeth. It almost seemed like she would keep it as a prize, as a trophy. She looked deep into Rommond's eyes, and he knew immediately that she wanted what he desired: to finish Domas once and for all.

"Clear the room," Rommond ordered to his troops. They left without question.

"Can't have any witnesses?" Domas taunted. "Don't tell me you're about to do something … inhumane."

They ignored him, even though he continued to taunt them as they spoke.

"I want this honour," Rommond said.

Taberah shook her head violently. "No. He's mine. I didn't spare him. My weapon did."

"Domas is part of the reason why Brooklyn isn't here any more," Rommond said. "I think I deserve this chance at vengeance."

"You're not the only one who lost," Taberah cried. "Domas *raped* me, Rommond! The first year when they came. I didn't even know they were demons at the time. Brogan is *his* child. Every time I look at him, every time I see the boy, I see Domas in his eyes. Don't you dare tell me I don't deserve this kill!"

Rommond bowed his head. "I'm sorry," he said. "I did not know."

"I wanted to tell you," she said, "so many times. But I didn't want *anyone* to know."

They heard a sound at the door, which was slightly ajar. Though they did not see who it was that had been eavesdropping, they knew from the fleeing shadow, short and thin, that it was Whistler.

Chapter Twenty-five

MONSTER

Whistler retreated to his room, and sat on his bed, clutching the small mirror Doctor Mudro had given him. He was supposed to check and replace his bandages regularly, but often he did this without looking in the mirror. He did not like what looked back.

He often rubbed his fingers across his face, to feel if he was growing any hair upon his upper lip. How he imagined proudly bearing a moustache like that ferocious one that Rommond bore, and how he then dreamed of stubble on his chin, like that chopped forest on Jacob's face. And then he would be a man, and the whiskers might weigh down his lip and make him a quieter man, one less prone to say childish things, one less likely to speak of secret things.

A man.

But now he looked upon his smooth face, and instead of a first fuzz he saw the faded scars, and he wondered if any hair might ever grow there. Bandages were still taped to his cheeks, which were even now somewhat tender, and he feared to take them off. He trembled at the thought of what might be written in the blotches of his skin.

How could he ever be a man, when he was, at best, half-human? He feared that instead of growing up to be a man, he would grow into a monster. The blood of the Regime in him would take hold, and he would betray willingly those he betrayed accidentally before.

He cried, and he berated himself for crying, for proving to himself that he was still a boy, a child with childish hopes and fears.

He understood then why he could sense the demons, how he knew when some of them infiltrated the Order. It was not just some uncanny skill. They were his kin.

Jacob found Whistler in his room, staring at the small oval mirror, with half the bandages ripped off his face. In the mirror Jacob could see the scars and blotches that covered much of the right side of the boy's face.

"I'm a monster," Whistler whispered, as if he did not want to hear those condemning words. Undoubtedly they were louder in his mind.

"You're not," Jacob said.

"I'm a monster!"

"It's just a few scars, kid. I've had worse. They'll heal in time."

Whistler stared at himself in the mirror. Perhaps he saw a monster staring back.

"It's not just the scars," Whistler said, though clearly they bothered him too. "It's …"

Jacob was not surprised that he could not continue. He was there with Whistler at the door, listening in, and as he listened he knew he should have been keeping the boy away. It was too late for that now. The secret was out, and though Domas was likely to die that night, it was certain that his ghost would haunt them all.

"My … my father," Whistler stuttered, "was a *demon*, so that … that means I must be part-demon too. How can I not be a monster then?"

Jacob sighed. "Look, kid. It doesn't matter who your father was, or what were the circumstances of your birth. Your blood runs through your body, not your personality. You're a good kid, Whistler. Good kids just can't be monsters. It doesn't work like that. Hell, there's more monster in me, and both my parents were human."

Whistler was not so easily consoled, and Jacob could not blame him. It would have taken the words of a higher being to reach through the darkness, and Jacob was no angel. Yet despite this, despite his almost certainty that he spoke in vain, that his words fell on deaf ears, that they touched a frozen heart, he continued.

"You know, kid, I've been thinking about this a lot lately. I'm not sure they really are demons. They come from somewhere else, sure, and some of them, many of them, do some pretty evil things, but I'm not convinced they're all like that. I think we call them demons because we want to justify our hate, and maybe hate just isn't justifiable."

Whistler paused mid-sob, as if now his tears had frozen. "I don't want to hate them," he said.

"Then don't hate."

"I don't want to hate myself," the boy continued.

Jacob placed his hand upon Whistler's shoulder. "Then don't hate."

Whistler looked back at the mirror, where the monster hid behind a mask of bandages, and behind a human mask.

"It'll heal," Jacob promised. "Trust me." He showed Whistler a faint scar that ran down his left forearm. "I usually tell people I got this in the trenches, but the truth is I slipped while climbing over a wall, and got caught on the barbed wire. Smuggling's a dangerous business, after all. And look, you can barely notice it now."

Whistler forced a smile.

"It'll heal," Jacob repeated. He patted Whistler on the back. "I'll get the doctor to apply some fresh bandages," he added before heading out of the room.

"You have to deal with Brogan," Rommond told Taberah.

She shook her head violently. "First, I deal with this demon here."

"You can't ignore the boy forever, Tabs."

This time she ignored Rommond's words. She looked at Domas squirming on the ground, barely able to muster a smug smile, and yet looking like he was enjoying dying as much as he enjoyed living. In death, he got to do what he did in life: ruin the lives of others.

"It's time," she said. She looked into Rommond's eyes. He saw many years of buried pain there, too many to count. How many occasions had she said *It's time*, only for Domas to once again slip through the net? Rommond knew the hurt, and the hatred. That was how he knew that this time, no matter what, Domas had to die.

Rommond took out his pistol and handed it to Taberah.

"Is it loaded?" she asked.

"Freshly."

"Do you mind if I spend the lot?"

"Spend away."

There were no smiles shared. The executioner does not revel in the job. What must be done is done. A life taken, for a life taken. Rommond knew as he watched Taberah raise the gun, that just like him, she was alive, but was not living. This war had claimed so many of their friends and comrades, and though they yet lived, it had claimed them too.

"So, you've come to say goodbye," Domas said.

She said it with her gun.

Whistler did not budge from his seat for the entire time Jacob was gone, which was probably only fifteen or twenty minutes, but felt like a lifetime—a lifetime where Whistler never grew up, stayed at that halfway point between boy and man, and between human and demon.

He peeled off more of the bandages. Some came off with ease, but others clung to his tender skin, and he cringed and yelped as he pulled at the strips. Part of him did not want to see, but the other part *had* to see. He had heard of the mummified remains of the Treasury's ancestors, buried with their vast kingdoms of gold, and tomb thieves were rampant then, and still active now, taking everything they could, even the brittle bones. Some said they were cursed, and that any who dared defile their tombs would know an evil fate. When the bandages were undone, they glared out at all, horrifying all, and beckoning all to join them in death. All of those images, those thoughts and teachings, flashed in Whistler's head, until he almost felt that he unearthing his own tomb.

Then Whistler heard a noise in the room, like a footstep, and he feared that he had summoned something from those ancient crypts, that dwelling on their memories had called them back to the land of the living where they could be remembered even more.

He was afraid to turn around, but he mustered the courage to do so. There was no one there.

"Jacob?" he asked, his voice wavering.

Silence seemed to be his only companion. Even the echoes fled.

"Is that you, Jacob?" Whistler asked again, when he heard the creak of the floorboards. He thought he saw a shadow pass by the door, and he suddenly felt like he was not alone. Though he had sobbed about his solitude, he would rather have that now.

Then he thought he heard a whisper, and though he could not make out the voice, he could make out the words: "Sometimes it's more fun to be a monster."

Chapter Twenty-six

THE BRIG

The battle with the Regime was over, and all of its submarines were destroyed or disabled. The Lifemaker limped through the waters, running at half power, and all but one of the air tanks were depleted. It should have been six months' supply, but it was only three months in, and half of the supply was lost to tampering, which Rommond blamed on Karlsif, though the cook only claimed responsibility for damaging the ballast tanks.

There were few Regime soldiers left alive at the end of the fight, and Rommond interrogated them all, and shot most of them when they showed they had no useful information. At one time he believed in honouring the enemy's surrender, in the unwritten rules of war. No longer. He kept a single prisoner alive, not as a point of honour, but because he was one of the planners behind the attack, and Rommond wanted to know how the Regime had found them.

The man, who refused to tell his name, and was known among the Resistance as Demon X, was locked in the Lifemaker's brig, where he continued to defy Rommond, where he continued to remind Jacob of his childhood in the workhouse prisons, and of his later time in the Hold, and of Whistler's longer stay. The man before him might have been a demon, but it was hard for Jacob not to feel something for him, to want to see him free.

"Do you have a man on board?" Rommond asked.

"We do now," the captive replied with a grin.

Rommond gritted his teeth. "*Did* you have a man on board before the attack?"

He was greeted with silence, and a broad smile.

"Co-operate, and we will let you live."

"We know all about you, Rommond," the man responded. "If I co-operate, you will let me die."

Rommond drew close to the bars. "Maybe you will think that is mercy soon enough."

"You used to have honour," the demon said.

"I used to do a lot of silly things," Rommond replied. "I used to love. You, *all of you*, took that from me."

"We used to talk about you in the trenches," the prisoner mused aloud. "*He ain't half as bad as he's cracked up to be. He ain't the monster Domas makes 'im out to be.* What happened?"

"What happened?" Rommond shouted, grabbing the bars. "I'll tell you what happened! I got a letter. *Give up or Brooklyn dies*, they threatened. *We can't give up*, I said. We all said it. We even said Brooklyn would say it too. Then I got one of his fingers in a box. In a *puzzle* box. It took me hours just to get it open. It was harder to say anything then. So I said nothing, and we all said nothing, and maybe I kidded myself by thinking Brooklyn would say nothing too. Then I got his hand, his right hand, in another puzzle box, and I knew it was his hand. I recognised it, recognised the markings. How long I held that hand when he was living. How long I held it still when he was dead. But he wasn't dead yet, and I prayed, prayed to his gods, to his spirits, to his ancestors, that the Regime would show him a little of the mercy I showed to so many soldiers. I got one more letter, threatening to send his head. What could I do? Even if I gave up, if I stopped fighting and handed myself in, chances were they'd kill him anyway."

"Stop," the prisoner objected. "I didn't mean to bring all this up."

"No," Rommond said. "You asked, and now I'm answering. You wanted to know why. This is why. I sent them a letter back, asking for the head of the Iron Emperor instead. God, I wish I hadn't sent that letter. But it probably wouldn't have mattered. They sent another box, another puzzle box—a bigger box—and the letter accompanying it just said: *You wanted to see him, face to face.* I tried to open the box, but I couldn't. I couldn't see him like that! So I buried his dismembered parts in a patch of grassland near where his people lived, perhaps the only sacred ground left on this unholy earth.

"So, if you think I have no honour, ask what honour was in what they did to him. Ask how this invasion has any honour. Even if you were my fellow man, to me you will always be demons."

"I wasn't party to those acts," the prisoned objected. "I didn't kill Brooklyn."

"And what were you planning to do here? If he

were still alive, your actions, your plots and schemes, could have killed him now all the same. How many of our people have died from this attack? How many of our women, those few who can continue our race, have fallen to your gunfire? Don't you dare berate me about honour! I knew honour in my heart and soul. You only know the word."

Rommond withdrew and turned towards the door. "If he won't talk," he said, "then let him starve."

"I thought they were supposed to be the demons," Jacob said.

"This is war, Jacob, and it's not a war over territory or principles. It's a war for the survival of humanity. These demons parade about, pretending to be us. But they are nothing like us. They take. They consume. Our world is a giant feast to them, and, by all gods, this demon won't take another crumb until he helps us first."

"What if he doesn't know anything?"

"And what if he knows something that could help us turn the tide? He planned this attack. He knows how they found us. And maybe if he knows our weaknesses, he can tell us his own."

"Surely he would be more willing to talk," Jacob said, "if he wasn't starved."

"You know my mind on this," Rommond stated. "If no words will come out, then no food will go in."

Rommond stormed out, slamming the door shut behind him, as if to lock Jacob in as well. The guards outside the door did not budge or flinch. They were the perfect statues that the general had carved them into.

Jacob looked around the room. He was alone with the prisoner. Somehow he felt more at home inside that small room, almost locked away. It was such an odd thing to yearn for freedom when imprisoned, but then to yearn for the comforts of the cage when freedom is granted. The wide, empty deserts of Altadas diminished the value of freedom, and yet Jacob felt that even if it were just a concept, he would still fight for it.

"I tried," he told the prisoner.

"I saw."

"This is his ship."

"I know."

Jacob sighed.

"We're not monsters," the man said. He looked even less monstrous behind those bars. Jacob imagined how a nightmare might have seemed defanged by being locked up, subdued and subjugated. He knew well that looks could be deceiving, however.

"Well, you didn't exactly come from Heaven," Jacob said.

"We didn't come from Hell either."

"Where did you come from, then?"

"A beautiful world, more beautiful than this one."

"Then why did you come here?"

"We were stricken with famine," the demon said. "Our world could no longer support us. It became an empty husk. It forced us out."

"So you invaded ours?"

"It wasn't supposed to be an invasion. That's not what the Iron Emperor promised us."

"What did he promise?" Jacob asked.

"Iron."

"Well, you got that, along with human lives."

"Iron is the bedrock of our civilisation. We need it to survive."

"And now it's the bedrock of mine, and the lining of every wallet."

"We didn't mean to cause all this destruction."

"I have a hard time believing that," Jacob said. "And I doubt Rommond would buy it either."

"I'm not surprised he hates us."

"You do make it easy to hate."

"Do you always talk to those you hate?"

"Well, I'm not entirely sure I hate *you*. I don't like what the Regime has done. Then again, you've given me a job. Hell, you've given the entire Resistance a job."

"A mission."

"Well, you're wiping us out," Jacob noted.

"We didn't intend to."

"It doesn't matter."

"It does," the prisoner objected. "Because you do intend to wipe us out."

When Jacob left the brig, he found it difficult to return. For one, Rommond put extra guards on duty, who were ordered to refuse all visitors. Jacob thought the general might have especially prohibited him from entering. He also was not sure if he really wanted to go back. It was easier to fight for "the cause" if the enemy was not in chains, and if the enemy did not share his own side of the story.

Several days passed where Jacob tried to keep

himself busy. The prisoner's only visitor was an interrogator, who always left more unhappy than he entered. Perhaps the prisoner was threatened. Perhaps he was even tortured. He certainly was not fed. Jacob found his own form of torture in thinking about these things, and feeling that he was somehow a silent accomplice. As each day passed, he felt a little more inhuman for having done nothing.

On the fifth day of the prisoner's incarceration, Jacob went back to the brig during the night, making sure to stay out of anyone's way. He tried to avoid mischief, while knowing well that Rommond would think his skulking activity was a mischief of its own. He smuggled a sandwich with him, a small act of compassion he felt he had to make for the starving prisoner, and, unlike the amulets, he did not intend to charge a fee.

The night watch was lax, and the guard was missing. One man's negligence was Jacob's convenience. He slipped into the brig with ease. He placed the plate down on the table opposite the prison bars, aware that it might have looked like he went there just to have a mocking midnight feast.

"Keep this quiet," Jacob whispered, "and I'll smuggle in some more."

He turned to view the prisoner, expecting some reluctance and defiance, the kind of qualities he knew he would have had if their roles had been reversed. But there was no one there. Instead, there was a monstrous hole in the cage, as if the hungry captive had eaten through the bars.

Chapter Twenty-seven

SABOTEUR

"Who let him out?" Rommond growled, when he arrived after the alarm was raised.

Blame immediately fell on Jacob, despite his fervent protests. Even Taberah came to him privately to ask if he did it, promising she would not tell, while perhaps keeping her fingers crossed behind her back. Jacob was not sure she believed his denial. Had he been a detective instead, he knew he would have picked himself as the prime suspect too.

"I'm telling you, I didn't do it," Jacob said as the interrogator turned to him. He seemed more pleased with this turn of events, which undoubtedly distracted him from his failure to elicit any useful information from the prisoner.

"The guard found you in the brig."

"With a sandwich," Jacob said. "Maybe I used it to cut through the bars."

"We should lock him up," the interrogator said as he turned to Rommond.

"Where?" Jacob asked. "The brig's kind of not that secure."

"We could confine you to quarters," Rommond suggested.

"Hell, Rommond, are you going to starve me as well? Who's the real demon on this submarine?"

Rommond sighed. "Let him go."

"But he's dangerous," the interrogator objected.

"I said let him go."

The interrogator reluctantly agreed, and Jacob got up and strolled towards the door.

"Jacob," Rommond called back. "Try to stay out of trouble."

Jacob smiled. "I'll try." Trying was easy. The problem was that trouble had a way of finding him.

Jacob headed back towards his quarters, halting every now and then to look behind him. He had the distinct feeling that someone was following him. He listened for a while, but heard nothing. *I hope I'm not getting paranoid*, he thought. Yet it was just like Rommond to have him followed, to see if he really was behind the breakout.

He reached his room and paused at the door, looking down the corridor on either side. No one was around. Even Whistler was not nearby. Jacob wondered if the general had ordered him to stay away.

He entered his quarters and lay down on the bed. Everything aboard the Lifemaker was becoming too much. He had not signed up for this. He had not signed up for anything at all. He wondered if now that there was only a month's air supply left, Rommond might issue orders for the submarine to surface soon. Then maybe Jacob could get out, could get away from all the turmoil, all the accusations. He seemed to be fighting with and for the Resistance, but they never afforded him any trust. With so many betrayals, he could not honestly blame them.

He felt restless, and he knew the best cure for that, the best way to quiet his mind. For some it was alcohol, and others Hope. For him, it was counting coils. He got up and pulled the crate from under his bed. He opened the lid and began to rummage inside. The feel of the metal, the cold iron, was so very reassuring. He squatted down beside the crate and began to count the coils, arranging a pile of them on the floor.

Then he heard a footstep behind him, and there was something familiar about it, something revealing in its rhythm, but before he had a chance to turn around, he was struck on the head with a blunt object. The pain was quick and sudden, but the darkness was quicker. He collapsed to the ground in body, and his mind collapsed into nothingness.

When Jacob awoke, the pain had returned in force. What he did not feel when he was unconscious, he felt now multiplied, as if all the aches were saved and stored for that moment of waking. He groaned as he tried to open his eyes, and grimaced as the light from the oil lamp attacked them. He could not see much; everything was a blur of shadows and silhouettes, and while his eyes were adjusting, he began to notice his other senses. He could feel that he was sitting down on a hard wooden chair, and he could feel that his arms and legs were tied to it. He tried to move them, but the bonds were tight. He could hear a minute metal sound, and he could have sworn it was like someone flicking a coil into the air. He wondered if it was just his mind seeking out something familiar, something comforting. It was the smell, however, that struck him the strongest. Perfume. Not a sweet, delicate smell, but a strong, pungent one. There was something familiar about that smell.

He heard a voice emanating from the silhouette ahead of him. "Wakey, wakey," it said.

Jacob responded with a groan. He tried to strain his hearing. The voice was also somewhat familiar, but it was muffled and warped by the ringing in his ears.

"Wakey, wakey, Jakey boy."

The figure came closer, out of the shadows, and it was unmistakable who it was: Cala. She stood before him, hand on hip, flicking a coil into the air, and smiling her famous smile, the kind of smile that said she was about to have a lot of fun.

"You," Jacob grumbled.

Cala gave a mocking curtsey. "The one and only," she said. "You look surprised to see me."

"Maybe it's less surprise and more disappointment."

Cala's smile soured. "Don't be like that, Jake. You're spoiling the mood."

Jacob tugged at the ropes that kept him in place. "I think this spoils enough."

"You never used to complain," she replied with a grin. She came closer and sat on his lap, and stared into his eyes, as if she could tie them up too. "You even said you liked it."

"We're not together any more!" Jacob shouted.

"Right then!" Cala replied, clambering off him and stamping her heels into the floor. She often wore platform boots. Jacob was not sure if it was to make her taller or if she just liked the feel of them. She was always unpredictable.

Jacob looked around for anything he might be able to grab to cut himself free. He could not tell exactly where he was, but he knew it was not his room. As he glanced about, he saw a body slumped in the corner, half-hidden in the shadows. It was the prisoner.

"Why did you set him free if you were just going to kill him?" Jacob asked.

"To see how you'd all react," Cala said. "I was going to let him wander the ship and cause some damage, but he wouldn't do it. He was no fun. So I killed him."

"Is that what you'll do to me?"

"Depends if you play or not."

"First, tell me how the hell you tracked me here."

"You've never been hard to find, Jake," Cala responded.

"Even ten thousand leagues under the sea?"

"Even deeper."

"I'm glad you don't work for the Regime."

"I don't really work for anyone, Jake. I play. Life is the biggest game."

"You can't win life."

"No, but you can have a lot of fun while playing."

She flicked a coil over to Jacob. He would have caught it if his hands were not bound. It struck him in the face and landed on the floor. The light was dim, but he could see the strange markings on it. It was the same coil that Whistler had discovered earlier, the one that did not bear the icon of the Iron Emperor.

"So, what's this?" he asked. "You looking to topple the Iron Emperor and put your own image there?"

Cala cackled. "Hardly. Though I guess that would be kind of fun as well. But Jake, baby, that's not a *real* coil."

"Well, it wouldn't be accepted most places, sure."

"No, Jake. It's a tracking device. You're not the only one can smuggle things, you know. When I saw you in Blackout, I kept watch from the shadows. And when they started loading up the truck, I snuck one of those little beauties into every crate."

"That explains a lot," Jacob said. He tried to crush the device beneath his foot.

Cala giggled. "Like that matters now. I already found you again."

"With tricks and toys."

Cala smiled broadly. "Oh, you should see the toys the Brigade has."

"Stolen, no doubt."

"Who cares?"

"The people they stole them from."

"God, Jake, when did you start caring about them?"

"I'm not the man I used to be."

"So you say, Jake, baby, but I think that's all a mask. I think you just need a reminder of who you really are beneath. That's partly why I'm here."

"How did you get on the Lifemaker?"

"The same way you did, Jake. I walked on.

Security wasn't exactly tight. With all the fuss of the evacuation, it was easy to smuggle aboard. When I tracked you to Dustdelving, I just couldn't pass up an opportunity like that, to see the deeps, to watch you from the shadows, to get to feel what it must be like to be a ghost, haunting everyone. And it was fun at first, until I started getting bored. So I thought we all needed a little excitement. A few holes here and there in the air tanks would do. God, Jake, you should have seen the panic."

"I did see it. I was there for it all."

"And didn't it make all the boredom go away?"

"I wasn't bored before that," he said, though he knew this was not entirely true. He was seeking out adventures and mischief of his own; it just did not involve the possibility of sinking the submarine.

"You're a liar, Jake, and I see right through you! Your mask might work for all these military types, but you and I both know who you really are beneath. You're a scoundrel, Jake. You grew up in the filth like I did. You know what it's like to slum it, and there's no amount of fancy cushions and curtains will cover up who you really are. You like the *raw* life, the *true* life, the *real* life. No pretences. No *how-do-ya-do's*. That's why you can go around climbing that swanky social ladder and you'll still want to climb back down to where I am."

"I'd rather go to Hell," Jacob said.

"Then let's go there, baby Jake," she replied, and her earnestness was unsettling. "Let's go down so deep we can *never* get back up again. All the gold and iron might be at the top of one ladder, but all the fun is at the bottom of another."

Jacob shook his head. "You're crazy."

"I suppose you think disconnecting the air tanks is crazy. I call it good fun."

"Hell, Cala, you're going to kill us all!" Jacob shouted.

Cala shrugged.

"Are you serious?" Jacob asked. "You don't care if you die?"

"It's gotta be more fun than the life you're living, Jake."

"You really are insane."

Cala shrugged again. "I'm good fun though, amn't I? And that's all that matters."

"It's not," Jacob said. "Life matters. Hell, Cala, I've got a kid on the way."

Cala turned away and clenched her fists. "Is that with that wench Tabby? I've seen her, strutting around the place. She doesn't love you, Jake. No one here loves you like I did. No one here gave you what you really needed, what you really wanted. *I* gave you that, Jake. *I* did."

"That wasn't life, Cala. That was something to cover up the pain."

She looked to the side and bit her lip. "I just want the good ol' days back, Jake."

"There weren't any good days back then," Jacob replied. "It was all bad."

"Not to me," she said, snuffling up some Hope. "They were the best times."

"Those drugs have messed up your memory then."

"No, they've made it clearer," she said. "It's you who isn't remembering right. You go on as if I was just some passing interest, some little dot on your sonar!" She banged her fist on the metal wall. The sound echoed out into the nearby chambers. "I matter, Jake. I matter!" she continued. "That's what you seem not to understand. You think I'm just some wacko, coming in here shouting my head off. But I'm more than that. That's what the Brigade is all about. Making people listen. Making people wake up, wake up from the dream of life. If no one gives you their ear, you've got to blow it off!"

"That group is dangerous," Jake said. "You shouldn't—"

"*I'm* dangerous, Jake. I want you to realise that. I want to be able to stand in the shadows and you'll still see me."

"Well, you've got my attention, Cala, but it's not the right kind of attention."

"Does it matter?"

"Yeah, it kind of does."

"Not to the ignored."

"I didn't ignore you, Cala. We broke up. We went our separate ways. That was years ago. Haven't you moved on? I mean, look at what you're doing here. This is madness."

"Jake, what'd you be doing right now if I didn't have you tied to this chair? Nothing, that's what! Absolutely nothing. I've been watching you for ages now. Ages! Sure, Jake, you ain't even got a job on this ship. You're more like a fancy, prissy passenger on this diesel diver."

"And what are you?" Jacob asked.

"I'm the iceberg in all yous'r way."

"Sink this ship, and you'll sink with us."

"I know that, Jake," Cala said. "I'm not dumb! Wasn't the trip to the abyss fun? God, the panic! It was a riot! And I mean that both ways, Jake, both ways. You know, I always wanted to see what was down there. And I didn't really get a proper look last time, so, hey, if we go down again, while yous'll all be shutting up your eyes real tight, I'll have mine *wide* open!"

"For what, a minute or two? We'll either drown, suffocate, or be eaten."

"But isn't death exciting?"

"Hell, Cala, you're even more a lunatic than I remember!"

Cala shook her head. "You're not remembering very well, Jake. You used to go along with all this. You used to come up with half the thrills." She took another hit of Hope. "Uh! We used to destroy the place. This world … it was *always* a desert to us. We were the demons back then."

"And it looks like you still are," Jacob said.

"And what, Jake, are you an angel now? You shack up with your little carrot-haired friends and suddenly you've earned your halo? If there really is a Hell, Jake, you're coming right down with me!"

She climbed onto his lap again. She leant real close, close enough to kiss him. He could taste the Hope on her lips, and tried to spit it out.

"Don't be wasting it!" she said. "That's good stuff, that."

"Get off me," Jacob struggled, but the bonds kept him firmly in place.

She took a little Hope on her finger and passed it in front of Jacob's nose, making aeroplane noises as she went. "Come on, Jake, baby Jake, gotta take your medicine. Breathe, baby, breathe!"

Jacob held his breath and kept his mouth closed. But she was just as stubborn as he was, and his face went blue as he tried desperately not to breathe in the drug.

"Oh, we've gotta a bluer!" she cried, shouting to the shadows of the room, who seemed more interested than ever. "That's the way, Jake. Hold before Hope, blue before white." She waved the white substance back and forth between his nose and mouth, waiting for one of them to take the influx of air.

Finally Jacob could not hold his breath any longer, and he gasped for air. She shoved her finger in his mouth, and he coughed and spat, and his tongue lolled, and his teeth clenched, but already he could taste the bitter substance, and already Cala was cheering him on.

"Go, baby, go!" she cried. "That's the way. Give in to it. Don't fight it. Don't fight me. You never used to fight me. Give in. Let go, baby Jake. Let go."

But Jacob fought. He fought the outer battle with Cala, whose Hope-fuelled muscles overpowered him, and he fought the inner battle with the drug, which coursed through the veins of his own muscles, and entered his brain, a little invasion of its own.

"I don't want your drug!" Jacob roared as she forced him to take some more.

"This whole vessel's a drug," she said. "It's better than an eyebox. Better than poppin' and shootin' and slippin'. We're inside the needle here, Jake, inside the capsule. We're so far down, we just gotta get high!"

She forced more of the drug into his mouth, then gagged him with his handkerchief. He couldn't spit the powder out, and he tried for a long time not to swallow it, but it lingered on his tongue and in his teeth, and it tasted foul and acerbic, like iron. He knew it was only a matter of time before it seeped into his bloodstream.

Suddenly Jacob heard someone at the door. Then he heard Whistler's voice. "Jacob," he called. "Is that you, Jacob? Are you in there?"

No! Jacob thought. *Go back, kid. Go back, for God's sake.*

But Whistler did not go back. He stepped cautiously into the room, glancing back and forth between Jacob, tied up and gagged, and Cala, who smiled warmly at him. "What's going on?" he asked.

"We're playing a game," Cala told him.

Jacob tried to speak, but the words were muffled. *Get out of here, kid. Run!*

But Whistler did not run.

"What kind of game?" he asked hesitantly. He took another step forward.

"I call it *Tickle the Liar*," Cala said. "And Jake likes being tickled."

"Why is he tied up?"

"He doesn't know he likes being tickled."

"Umm, okay," Whistler said.

"Come on in and I'll show you how it's played."

"I think I'll just watch," Whistler said, taking a step back.

"It's no fun just watching," Cala said, and her smile faded. "You've got to get involved."

"Why has he got his mouth covered?"

"He laughs so much when I tickle him," Cala explained. "He can be very loud."

"I think I'll go and—"

"Wait, boy," Cala said. "I can tell that you're an outsider. A loner. Don't you want to hang out with people just like you?"

Damn it, Jacob thought. He knew that if she had been stalking him all this time, she likely knew of Whistler's fears and doubts, and could easily exploit them.

"What's your name, boy?" Cala asked.

"Whistler."

"Is that your real name?"

Whistler hesitated. "No."

"Well, you can be whoever you want to be. You can choose your own name. Sure, you can have a different name for every hour of the day. People usually call me Cala, but we've got to escape all these labels. Regime this, Resistance that. Why can't we just be whoever we want? Why can't we just drift between all these boundaries?"

"I suppose," Whistler said.

"You don't have to work for them, you know."

Whistler stared at her, but said nothing.

"You don't have to be their dog, barking when they tell you to. You can be a free soul like me and Jake here. We just come and go as we please. We do our own thing. No rules. No orders. We just have our fun, and that's all."

Jacob mumbled a warning. *Don't listen to her, Whistler*, he tried to say. But Whistler was already listening.

"You don't have to stay here, boy," Cala continued, pushing a different kind of hope. "You don't have to be here with Rommond and all his rules, or Tabby and her schemes. This is a prison. I'm helping Jake here break out. Do you want me to get you out too?"

The offer must have been tempting, Jacob thought, and it must have reminded him of the Hold, and how long it took for Taberah to rescue him, and how that even now that he was rescued, she seemed not to notice him at all.

"No one here cares about you," Cala said bluntly.

Whistler looked at Jacob, who tried to mumble a response. *I care*, Jacob thought. He hoped his eyes spoke enough.

"Don't look at him. He doesn't care about you. He only cares about money. He was the same way with me. The only thrills he ever went for were the ones that resulted in a quick buck, or the ones that were cheap. I didn't realise it back then, but I've got the 'piphany about it now. I know all about him now." She stabbed the side of her head several times with her finger, pointing out where the knowledge was.

Then Cala began patting Jacob's face, as if trying to wake him up, but he was already frightfully awake. The drug was beginning to kick in. His vision sharpened. It seemed like he was seeing things for the first time, and seeing too much. All the lines and pores on Cala's face were visible, like a map.

"You know, boy," Cala continued, waving her hand at Whistler, who stood like one of Rommond's statues, paralysed by the display before him. "There's all sorts out there. There's uppers and downers. Jake here, baby Jake, he's a downer. Doesn't wanna know what it feels like. Doesn't wanna live. But this, here, this is an upper!" She held up the bag of Hope, held it up to Heaven, as if praising whatever god she believed had created it. "This makes all the doubt and fear and pain go away."

Jacob's mind felt like it was speeding up and slowing down simultaneously. He felt he could follows several lines of thought at once, and yet could not concentrate long enough on any single one of them. When Cala's words finally processed in his brain, he looked at Whistler and saw more clearly than ever the doubt, the fear, and the pain. *Who wouldn't want it to all go away?*

"Jake here's had a go," Cala said. She drew close to Jacob and smiled. "Oooh! Looks like he's just getting started now. It isn't just the destination that's a hoot. It's all about the ride."

Whistler would not budge, and would not talk. Jacob wondered what was going on his mind, what new turmoil Cala had caused there, like she caused everywhere she went. Did Whistler ponder what the drug would be like? Did he want the freedom and fun that Cala promised, without her ever telling him of the horrors that came with it? Did he wonder if now that he knew he was part-demon, did he really need Hope to survive?

"There's no point in saying no," Cala said. "Let me make it easier for you."

"How?" Whistler asked.

"I've got the ballasts rigged," she said. "There's dynamite on all of 'em. And hell, if that doesn't kill us, all those holes I put in the air tanks will. So, you know what, boy, you might as well make it painless. If we're all going to Hell, and I'd bet all of Jake's money that we are, we might as well enjoy the way down."

Whistler's brow furrowed. Perhaps the horrors were clearer now.

"You don't belong here, boy," Cala said. "Kids are supposed to have fun, right?"

"I guess," he said reluctantly.

"Well," she said, holding out her hand to him, offering him the bag of Hope, and the promise of a new and more fulfilling life in its white powder, "sometimes it's more fun to be a monster."

Chapter Twenty-eight

HIGHS AND LOWS

Whistler reached for the bag of Hope that Cala offered him. To him she seemed so friendly and generous, so giving when so many others only thought of taking, but she talked a lot about masks, and he knew that this was one of her own.

Just as his hand was close enough to dip into the white powder, he whacked her hand and knocked the bag into the air. The powder leapt from it, spreading in all directions, and Cala leapt to catch it, but it went everywhere like a fine white snow. She dived to the ground, clutching the emptied bag and desperately clambering to fill it back up again.

"No!" she cried. "You're wasting it! You've wasted it!"

Whistler ran past her to where Jacob was struggling with his bonds, and clearly struggling against the drug. His eyes were freakishly wide, and his brow was covered in sweat. Whistler dared not think what was happening in his body, or in his mind.

The boy quickly untied Jacob's hands and feet, and removed the gag, and Cala might have lunged at them were she not frantically cupping and cradling every last granule of Hope upon the dirty floor. Some of this she scooped into the bag, but some she licked and snorted, until her hands trembled as she tried to save her drug.

"Look how low you've become," Jacob told her, but he struggled to keep his balance, and Whistler feared that he might fall and join Cala on the ground, hungry for another hit.

"Come on, Jacob!" Whistler said. He tried to help Jacob walk to the door, but he was too heavy. When Jacob stumbled in one direction, Whistler joined him, and it was only the wall that stopped them.

They hobbled over to the door, and Whistler had barely opened it when they heard Cala running towards them.

"No!" she screamed, and she threw herself at them, brandishing her nails.

They managed to get outside just in time, and Jacob slammed the door and turned the lock. They could see Cala through the small circular window, banging her fists against the door, pressing her cheek against the glass, staring out at them with her bulging eyes. She shouted and screamed, but they could not hear her, nor make out what she said.

"Sorry about that, kid," Jacob said, slurring his words.

"It's okay," Whistler said.

"I guess we've all got demons."

Whistler did not answer this. Jacob probably meant it to be reassuring, but Whistler did not like what he saw in Cala, or what he was seeing in Jacob. That this could happen to anyone scared him even more.

They stumbled a few steps down the corridor before Jacob collapsed upon the ground, pulling Whistler down with him.

"Go get help," Jacob said.

"I'm not leaving you."

"This is … more important than me. Warn the others."

"But—"

Jacob grabbed Whistler by the shoulder. "They have to get … up to air."

Whistler nodded reluctantly, and then raced off to alert Rommond.

Jacob thought he saw Whistler running in both directions at the same time, until he realised that the hall looked identical both ways, which did not match what he knew the layout of the submarine was like. The boy disappeared from view, and yet seemed to leave behind some kind of imprint, like a blur of motion that trailed behind like breadcrumbs.

"Hope you're not going mad," he said to himself aloud. He laughed. "Hope."

He hauled himself up until he rested his back more firmly against the wall. He noticed the strange pattern on the carpet beneath him, which stole his attention for a moment. Any time he moved, the pattern changed, and sometimes it felt like he was not moving at all, but everything else was moving around him. It was simultaneously unsettling and exhilarating.

"So soft," he said as he patted the carpet with both hands. The feeling was not just external. He felt as though everything inside of him was carpeted. All the aches and pains were cushioned. All the doubts and fears were softened. It took him a long time to realise that he was grinning and giggling to himself.

No! he thought. It almost did not sound like his own thoughts. *You've got to fight this. They're counting on you. You can't give in. You can't let go.* Yet just as he had slurred his words, he slurred his thoughts.

He tried to fight it, but it was harder than any physical battle. If he threw a punch, his fist just melded into the cushion he struck against, until all the anger and hate, all the force and strength, dissipated from his hand, and he did not even realise he was losing.

Then he heard a clink, and he smiled involuntarily. That was one of his favourite sounds, as reassuring as the sound of his heart beating. He heard it again, and then again, until it seemed that he was swimming in a giant pile of coils, all clinking together joyfully. He waved his arms through the fountain of iron currency, unaware that he looked like a madman to anyone around, and it all felt so wonderful, knowing that he would never be a slave to poverty again.

Then he heard a different sound: a loud alarm went off, and it was jarring, but then the sound began to shift and morph into other sounds, and then it was a rhythm, and he began moving his head to the beat, unaware of the droning monotone that everyone else heard.

Whistler might have run directly to Rommond were it not for him feeling guilty at leaving Jacob behind. He told the first guard he found about the dynamite in the ballast tanks, and then raced around until he found Doctor Mudro, who limped and puffed his way back to where Jacob was murmuring to himself.

"You weren't kidding," Mudro said. "He's had a heavy dose."

He held a bag of smelling salts up to Jacob's nose, and Jacob recoiled from them, but he appeared a little more alert than before.

"I need to give him Greenshield, a counteracting agent," Mudro explained. "It slows the absorption of the drug into the bloodstream, and alleviates many of the symptoms. See if you can get his mouth open."

Whistler struggled to open Jacob's mouth. The smuggler chomped playfully at him, laughing and turning his head this way and that, like an animal playing a game. Eventually he gave in and let Whistler hold his jaw wide.

Mudro poured a thick green liquid into Jacob's mouth, which the smuggler began to gargle and spit up immediately.

"Hold his nose shut," the doctor ordered. Whistler complied, and Jacob began to swallow the medicine, which Whistler could only guess was vile.

Mudro quickly packed up his things, for the surface alarm still raged around them. "That's the best I can do. The rest is up to nature. He just has to wait the course."

"But the ship is in danger," Whistler said. "We need to help him escape!"

"He'll regain much of his awareness and mobility pretty soon."

"And before then?"

Mudro took a puff on his pipe. "Let's hope the ship lasts that long."

Suddenly they heard a series of loud explosions at the back of the submarine, forcing everyone to stumble or fall inside. The intercom squeaked on.

"All hands," Rommond called out solemnly. "Abandon ship."

Chapter Twenty-nine

ASCENT

Water leaked into the stern of the submarine, and though the leak was small, it would not take long to fill the vessel, and bring them back down to the dark waters below. The Lifemaker rose rapidly through the waters, buoyed by the front ballast tanks, which were free of explosives. But this meant that the ship tilted upwards, making it harder for the people to work inside. Though one of the ballast tanks in the stern was destroyed in the explosion, the others were still intact—only because the dynamite sticks taped to them were diffused by the water that rushed into the room.

"Saved from one death by another," Rommond said coldly.

The front of the Lifemaker burst through the surface, like a bullet fired by an ocean gun. Had it any more power, it might have leapt into the air like a flying fish, and bore them away. Instead, it tilted forward and crashed back down upon the sea, sending enormous waves in all directions. It rocked there for a moment, and everyone inside it knew that they had less than a moment to get out before it sank again.

"Get the airship aloft," Rommond called out over the intercom. People ran frantically to and fro. No one really needed orders. Their instincts gave them orders to survive.

"All hands," Rommond's voice croaked over the speakers, grim and glum, as if the very Lifemaker had deserted him, "abandon ship. Repeat, abandon ship."

He ushered everyone bar Alson out of the command room. She bashed at the controls and tried to hold the ship steady. A wrong move now and it could overturn, preventing their means of escape.

"How long do you need?" he asked her.

"As long as you can give me."

"Ten minutes."

"That's not enough."

"It'll have to be."

He headed for the door, and she followed him. "I'm not leaving," she said, and shut it after him. She locked it tight, and she could see that he was shouting through the small round pane of glass. It looked like he was urging her to leave. She shook her head.

"You won't make it with no one at the wheel," she said, mouthing the words and hoping he would understand. "This is where I belong."

She returned to her station, which was every station now, and she heard Rommond trying to break down the door, slamming it with his shoulder, bashing it with a crowbar. She knew it would not budge. It was on Rommond's orders that those doors sealed tight, and nothing could break them down, not even him.

* * *

Two large hatches opened at the top of the submarine, exposing the people inside to the glaring sunlight, which they had not seen in months. They averted their gaze, and continued to work in the shadows below.

Doors were taken off their hinges, walls were knocked through, stairwells were moved like scaffolding on wheels, opening up a passage from the highest deck, exposed to the elements, to the lowest level, exposed to the flood of the sea.

The airship was pushed and pulleyed into place, and though it was not quite ready, it was now or never—and never was fast approaching. They hauled helium cannisters to the dirigible and pumped up the balloon enough for it to begin to take off of its own accord. It rose the length of the ropes that tied it down, and a wooden ramp was extended from the large main entryway down into the top deck of the Lifemaker.

Dozens raced up that ramp, which creaked beneath the load. The surviving Pure were bundled aboard the airship before any others, followed by anyone else not needed to transport essential cargo and supplies. It was a frantic race, and as many came back down the ramp to help as those who went up.

"The vehicles!" Rommond shouted. "Forget the cargo. Get the landships up!"

"That ramp won't hold," Boulder said.

Already the Copper Vixens began bracing it with metal rods and plates, nailing and riveting and soldering them in place, completing a week's work in minutes, never tiring and never resting, for fear of the eternal rest that threatened them all. Even as the last screw was turned, several landships sped up the makeshift metal ramp, which groaned beneath them.

Rommond raced through the submarine, shouting orders as he went. He could not tell who was coming or going, who was already aboard the airship, and who was drowning deep below. He passed by Taberah, who was helping some of the injured, and he passed by Jacob, Whistler, and Mudro, who limped and hobbled towards the airship.

Rommond ran to his quarters, where he yanked the plaque bearing Brooklyn's name from the wall. The screws that held it in place dropped to the cold ground like the dead. He looked around the room, at all the books and paintings he had collected, all the artwork he had saved, and he knew he had no time to collect or save them now. They would sink to the bottom of the ocean, joining the cache of culture in the Alda Kalta, that submerged museum that might one day house them all.

He left his quarters and raced down to the lower levels. He passed by many people, some he rarely saw in his normal course of duty. He halted when he came to the room where Cala still clawed at the door. He had no idea who she was, but he knew who she worked with, and what they were capable of. He took his master key from his belt and twisted it in the lock, sealing it in a way that could not be opened without that same key.

"There's someone in there!" one of the passing guards shouted.

"I know," Rommond said. He banged his fist

down and broke the key.

The general then continued down to the iron-works, which was already half-submerged in water. There were still many vehicles there, some that were being repaired, some that were being newly built. Some were even in working order, but the water was rising too rapidly. None of them could be saved.

Then the general saw that the Hopebreaker was among them, and he almost cursed aloud. Still clutching the plaque tightly, he climbed onto the landship's hull and hopped inside. He started it up and sped up the ramp to the next level of the submarine, and then the next, with the water rising behind him, until he reached the top deck, when the engine conked out. Too much water had already gotten inside.

If he did not care so much about that vehicle, he might have banged his fist upon the hull. Instead, he got up, popped his head through the hatch and glanced about until he saw Alakovi midway up the ramp leading to the airship. "Is this everything?" Rommond shouted up to her.

"That's all we can get," Alakovi roared back.

"Rommond!" Taberah called. She was helping the last of the survivors off the submarine.

He turned to her.

"The bomb," she said.

He looked down at the sinking vessel. "We'll have to leave it."

"Are you sure?"

He nodded solemnly. "It's probably for the best. Now get on!"

Taberah joined Jacob and the last of the crew who raced up the ramp to the airship. Rommond ducked inside the Hopebreaker and tried to start it up again. He felt it lunge, and he felt the submarine begin to sink more quickly beneath him. He took a deep breath, and hoped he would not have to hold it for eternity.

The Lifemaker was sinking fast, and many were fearful that the airship, which was still tethered to it, would go down with it. All eyes were on the Hopebreaker, but while some minds were with Rommond, many were focused on the greater threat to them all.

"Cut the ropes!" Boulder boomed outside.

"Not yet!" Taberah shouted back, but already one was frayed. "Give him a minute!"

Jacob bit his lip and shook his head. Mudro's magic was doing its trick, but Jacob's eyes were still dreadfully alert, so much so that he thought he could see every little drop of water that crept its way towards the Hopebreaker. *He's not going to make it*, he thought. Whistler dug his fingers into his arm.

The stern of the Lifemaker dipped below the waves, and the Hopebreaker slid down towards the back of the vessel, catching in a metal beam, the only obstacle keeping it from the rising waters. The submarine continued to dip, and the bow rose into the air, preparing it for its vertical plunge. It was clear that Rommond was struggling to get the landship moving. The tracks appeared to be jammed. He tried them forward, then reverse, and each time they caught. Each locked tread was another second closer to a grave beneath the sea.

"He should get out," Jacob said. "Swim for it, even. That landship will be like a leaden weight in the water. Why doesn't he just abandon it?"

"That was the last vehicle Brooklyn designed," Taberah explained. "He's not going to give it up that easily." She paused, as if she wished he would. "That's his pride and joy."

"It could also be his death."

Suddenly the treads clicked into place, and the Hopebreaker rolled slowly away from the metal beam. Yet the more it went, the more the submarine turned upright. The more the tracks struggled to keep grip, the more Rommond struggled to get the landship up towards the ramp, and the more everyone else struggled to keep watching.

"Come on, Rommond!" Taberah called, as if her cheer would help.

Come on, Jacob thought, as if that would help either.

The Hopebreaker pushed forward even more, and climbed the now forty-degree slope, but it still was not the ramp Rommond needed to climb if he was to get out to safety. The waters rose behind the landship, creeping closer to it, reaching out for one more victim. Rommond turned the vehicle sharply, and the tracks were now partly submerged. They spun like crazy, spraying water behind them, but there was less traction now, and the landship was more difficult to control.

"I thought the captain goes down with the ship," Soasa said.

Taberah glared at her. "He's not the captain."

You can do it, Rommond, Jacob thought, even as others were saying it out loud. People were cheering and shouting, and many were grimacing and averting their gaze.

The Lifemaker was now at fifty degrees, and it was dipping deeper and turning sharper. The Hopebreaker began to slide back down, and the waters were rising up around it, covering the treads entirely, almost making it a submarine of its own. But it was not designed to float.

The landship exhaled a tremendous amount of smoke, and it looked as though the very hull was sweating steam. How Rommond fared inside was anyone's guess, but they knew that he was giving it his all. They just hoped he would not have to give his life as well.

As the Lifemaker sank more rapidly, and the waters rose more quickly, the Hopebreaker powered through the water, sending the spray behind it, travelled precariously towards the airship, and thundered up the ramp.

"The ropes!" Boulder shouted. He sliced at the one nearest him.

"No!" Taberah cried.

The airship tried more earnestly to take to the skies, careening to one side and tugging on the remaining ties. The ramp began to come loose beneath it, and the Hopebreaker was still not fully up. The crew cried out in horror as the metal supports gave way, and as the wood snapped, and as the bolts abandoned ship. The landship rocked and tilted, and people bit their lips and closed their eyes. Then it continued on as the ramp collapsed beneath it, and entered the vehicle bay just in time as the last of the supports gave way.

The cheer that followed would have woke the gods. The remaining ropes were snapped, and the cheers died down into a depressing silence as the Lifemaker turned fully upright and sank deep beneath the waves. Some thought of Alson and her noble sacrifice. Some thought of Cala, and her ignoble deeds. Others thought of what might have been, how many might have died, how many were now saved. Others yet thought that their fabled refuge, that second home beneath the sea, was now gone. They hoped this third home within the clouds would bring them more luck, and less loss of life.

Rommond emerged from the Hopebreaker to applause, but he was not smiling. More than any, he clearly felt the loss of the Lifemaker, and those who had died aboard it. He did not stop their cheers, but he did not celebrate, and he held his cap to his chest, as if to hide the feelings of his heart.

He marched to his quarters and closed the door to the fanfare outside, and he did not come out again for hours. Some wondered if he was weeping. Some thought that maybe he was deep in prayer. Jacob mused that he was likely taking a well-deserved nap.

When the general came out again later that day, when the sun began to dip like a sinking vessel of its own, he climbed up to the highest part of the airship to get a better view. He took out an eyeglass and pointed it north-west, where he saw the plume of dark smoke that marked the city of Blackout.

"So, what's this one called then?" Jacob shouted up to him.

"It's what the people of Blackout will call it," Rommond said, climbing back down.

"What, Big Balloon?"

"No," the general said with a sigh. "It's what they will call it when we take back that city."

Rommond turned to Taberah, who looked as determined as ever.

"The Skyshaker."

About the Author

Dean F. Wilson was born in Dublin, Ireland in 1987. He started writing at age 11, when he began his first (unpublished) novel, entitled *The Power Source*. He won a TAP Educational Award from Trinity College Dublin for an early draft of *The Call of Agon* (then called *Protos Mythos*) in 2001.

His epic fantasy trilogy, *The Children of Telm*, was released between 2013 and 2014.

Dean also works as a journalist, primarily in the field of technology. He has written for *TechEye*, *Thinq*, *V3*, *VR-Zone*, *ITProPortal*, *TechRadar Pro*, and *The Inquirer*.

www.deanfwilson.com